Hi Mo
i he
the ..
best . love Phoebe
x

TIME IS OF THE ESSENCE

PHOEBE WILBY

Published by

Delahoyde Publishing Company Limited
First Published October 2017
Text & Graphic copyright © Phoebe Wilby,

2017

Wilby, Phoebe

Time is of the Essence

ISBN 978-0-473-41166-4 (Paperback)

ISBN 978-0-473-41168-8 (Kindle)

ISBN 978-0-473-41167-1 (Epub)

ISBN 978-0-473-41169-5 (PDF)

Contact Phoebe Wilby at Delahoyde Publishing Co Ltd at
Info@DelahoydePublishing.com

DEDICATION

To all the time travellers out there, making their journeys from birth to death and every destination in between, without you, there would be no stories.

Also by Phoebe Wilby

Point of View: It's all relative, really

Works in Progress

Discovering the Light –*Essays and articles exploring the personal journeys of real women of different faiths, religions and creeds and how they came to discover their own light within.*

Eden Trilogy
Exodus
The Genesis Protocol
Regeneration

Samara – Angel of the Morning

Read more of Phoebe Wilby's works at:
www.phoebewilbyauthor.com

Send her a message on
phoebewilbyauthor@gmail.com

CONTENTS

ACKNOWLEDGMENTS

Sometimes the second book is harder to get together than the first, and I have certainly found this to be true.

Still, I have the support of my mother (yes, a woman in her fifties still needs her mother), my husband, Ewen, and my children, Logan, Kurt, Hannah, Samuel and Rachel, whether still living at home or not. I thank you all for your continued support and encouragement.

I have also found a few mentors and helpers along the way that I would like to pay tribute to. Jennifer Blanchard for her incredibly informative and straight-talking writing blog, the staff at Starbucks who provide a fantastic working environment, allowing me to sit here with a hot chocolate or peppermint tea, plug in my laptop and get to work, and lastly to my good friend, Gina Sterling. Gina, your support and encouragement (and your begging me for my next book!) has helped more than you will ever know.

To all of you, thank you from the bottom of my heart.

SHORT STORIES

A Modern Fairy Tale

All fairy stories begin with the words "Once Upon A Time", and so we must begin...

Once upon a time there lived a princess. She was not an ordinary princess and she did not live in an ordinary castle with servants to do her every bidding. And although her daddy was a king, he had died a very long time ago, and her mummy, the queen, lived in another kingdom far, far away on the other side of the world.

Now our princess lived in a small house in a small market town in a small county of a small country which was once part of a huge and powerful empire, but which now governed only a very small portion of a much larger world.

On the outskirts of the small market town was a large expanse of land locals called the Moors, and it was here the princess would go when her less than regal life took a not unexpected turn for the worse. It was where she would pour out her soul to the trees, flowers and all tiny creatures, and although she never pretended to hear answers to her heartfelt cries, her time on the Moors always left her with a feeling of peace and the strength to keep going.

In a bigger town not far from the small market town where the princess lived, there lived a handsome prince. Now, as you may guess, he was no ordinary handsome prince. Although a native of this small, has-been empire, he was removed from his home at a young age and, only recently after many, many good and bad experiences, had made his way back, not to his home town, which was an icy palace somewhere up north, but to a balmy seaside naval town on the south coast.

****

High on a peak on the outskirts of the Moor stood what locals assumed was an old ruined chapel, and indeed, it was, until the sun set in the west and the stars struggled to shine through the perpetual mist. Then it was transformed and became the High Council, seat of the faerie folk.

Tonight was special. The air was particularly crisp and scented with wildflowers. Blossoms from the meadows below caught the currents and rose, dancing with delight to shower down upon the assembly. The faerie folk were out in their finery. Gossamer silk gowns, spider silk tights and blossom shoes, all in the natural shades of autumn, adorned the girls, while the menfolk dressed in the more robust tunics woven from fresh foliage. Their wings, both male and female, glittered with a thousand dewdrop gems and the women had intertwined blossoms and foliage through their hair. They were a glorious sight, and tonight they would crown their new king and queen.

Tallulah stood back from the assembly, watching and feeling the joy that everyone there basked in.

Pity I can't join in, *she thought, and her sigh was heavy. She had been given a task - a very special task, but so far, try as she might, she had failed. Somehow, she'd had to entice Prince Roderick to seek out Princess Annabel, fall in love with her and have her fall in love with him. And then he had to ask her to marry him. It was simple! Or so she thought when she had accepted her assignment during the final snow fall of the previous winter. The catch was, it all had to be done by tonight. Somehow, she had managed to get him to fall in love with her, but, well, Princess Annabel didn't know he even existed, and Prince Roderick was just too shy to introduce himself.*

****

Annabel was going to the ball!

It wasn't really a ball, just a dance to celebrate St Valentine's Day, albeit three weeks later. She didn't have anyone to go with. There was no longer a man in her life and her best friend and chief handmaid who had planned on going with her was very ill. Although Annabel felt she should have been by her side,

4

nursing her back to health, Charity had insisted she go.

"Have fun," she told her. "Lord knows you could do with it after all you've been through."

"Really?" One eyebrow lifted as Annabel looked at her friend over the top of the spectacles she wore for reading. "I'd rather curl up in front of the fire with a good book and a bar of chocolate. No glitzy St Valentine's Dance will ever top that for entertainment."

Charity took a momentary sidestep from living up to her name and scoffed.

"You'll never find yourself a prince with that lousy attitude."

"Maybe not, but at least I won't look desperate!"

Charity laughed. "Not desperate. No. But you do look pathetic."

"Thanks."

"You're welcome. Now trot off to ASDA and find yourself a ball gown."

It was after eight o'clock by the time she found something suitable to wear and, having nowhere handy to change, she managed to do it all in the front seat of her car. The gold top, black trousers and chunky jewellery didn't quite make her feel in a party mood but it was certainly better than the scrubs she had been wearing. A quick touch-up to her eye-liner and mascara, a flick of her brush through her luscious locks and she was ready to paint the town sultry.

She rocked up at the car park to the church hall just as Roderick climbed out of his chariot.

"Well. Hello!" he said. "Good timing." He grinned down at her.

"Oh. Well. Yeah. I guess so."

"Mind if I join you?"

"Erm. Er. No. Not at all."

They entered the Hall together.

****

Above them, hiding behind the glow of the street lamp, Tallulah watched. As the door swung closed, she flitted inside, heart pounding. Faerie folk didn't usually enter the places frequented by their giant earth-bound cousins, but she was anxious to see how this evening would pan out. A quick scan of the room revealed the perfect hiding place.

Red and silver tinsel streamers adorned the room, lowering the hall's ceiling by a good four or five feet. The room doubled as a sports hall and the basketball hoops had been given the same treatment and a huge red and silver heart balloon hung from each of them. Tallulah perched on a hoop, hiding behind the fronds of tinsel.

****

Annabel walked a little self-consciously beside the much taller Roderick. She knew who he was, of course. Recently divorced handsome Adonis of a man, tall, slim, blonde hair, blue eyes, and a hint of a beard. Just her type, really, except for the stories she'd heard. Still, he intrigued her.

A friend came up to her.

"He's here," she whispered.

"Really?" She shrugged. "Doesn't matter."

She glanced at Roderick, who didn't appear to have heard the exchange.

"Let's go this way," she said, gesturing toward the corridor that would take them to the other side of the hall and make their entrance less grand. He fell into step beside her and they entered the hall through the kitchen.

"Would you like a drink?"

"Yes, please." He handed her a plastic cup with some squash. It was gone in an instant.

She smiled up at him. "I was thirsty."

"Indeed! Shall we dance?"

He led her to the dance floor. Some modern pop was playing and they just moved to the music, not touching, not speaking. It would have been impossible to hear anyway. She glanced up and saw her ex looking her way. He was with his new wife, so why did he look like he wanted to be with her? She shook her head and turned away.

A slow song was playing. Awkward. Roderick held

out his hand.

"Shall we?"

She moved closer and was shocked by the warmth she felt as his arms encircled her, stiffening slightly, then relaxing as the shock gave way to comfort. She rested her head on his chest, and felt him rest his head gently on her hair.

"Your hair smells gorgeous," he whispered.

"Thank you," she said, breathing in the glorious manly smell of his aftershave and cologne, and she melted a little more into his arms.

The song ended and they drifted apart.

"I just need to use the ..." she gestured toward the door.

"I'll wait here."

She nodded and made her escape. Once inside, she leaned against the tiled wall, allowing the coldness to seep through her clothes to cool her down.

"Roderick seems to be stuck like glue to you tonight." Chrystal's soft voice broke into her reverie.

She shrugged.

"I don't mind. He's harmless."

"That's not what ..."

"I know, but what else would you expect an ex-wife to say?"

"You're an ex-wife..."

"Yep. And that's why I won't talk to her... don't want to accidentally say something I shouldn't ... must get back..."

Chrystal nodded. "So long as you're okay."

"I will be." She smiled. "I am."

She returned to the dance hall where Roderick handed her another drink.

"Thank you." She smiled again. "You're very thoughtful."

"You sound like you didn't expect that."

"No, it's not that. Let's just say it's refreshing."

He smiled as the DJ invited everyone up for the Virginia Reel.

"Shall we?"

"Why not?"

He led her to the dance floor and they joined in the mayhem that was the Virginia Reel, spinning wildly when it was their turn to dance up the middle. They were both breathless when it was over.

"That. Was. So. Much. Fun." She breathed.

They danced a bit more and eventually, the evening was winding up.

"I wasn't going to come, but thank you for such a great evening." It sounded so formal and stiff, but Annabel didn't know how else to say it.

"It was my pleasure." His eyes twinkled as he

looked into hers and she found herself swimming in the cool blue ocean. He walked her out to her car, arm loosely draped across her shoulders.

"We'll have to do this again."

"But it's a year until the next Valentine's Dance!" She looked up at him through her lashes. "You could maybe come for tea sometime."

"I'd like that."

He saw her into her car and watched as she pulled out of the parking lot.

****

"I've failed my task!" Tallulah flew toward Princess Annabel's retreating car in a panic. She stopped mid-flight and turned herself about. Sure she could go after the Princess, but where was she likely to be heading after her evening? Not home. Not yet. There was a place she always went when she wanted to talk things over and Tallulah knew just where she would be going. She darted back to the Prince.

"Prince Roderick," she whispered, flying just out of his line of sight, close to his ear. "You don't want to go home yet. Follow Princess Annabel. She may need your help."

****

Roderick swiped at an insect buzzing around his ear and the buzzing stopped. He sighed.

"I was so close," he muttered. "Maybe if I follow her home, we can continue this... whatever this is."

He leapt into his car, revved the engine, and sped off after her.

*****

Tallulah picked herself up off the ground where Prince Roderick had inadvertently swiped her and, snapping her fingers, re-appeared inside his car. She'd have to be a little more careful now. He didn't know his own strength.

*****

Roderick followed the route to Annabel's and was about to turn off the highway on to the road that would take him to her village when he noticed that a car very much like Annabel's was still on the road ahead. Intrigued, he decided to follow, to see if indeed it was her. It was easy enough to do this, unseen, while they were still on the main road, but as she headed further out of town turning left and right on to progressively smaller and less travelled roads, Roderick began to worry that she may have noticed she was being followed.

It was a needless worry. Annabel was too caught up in her own thoughts to notice the little sporty car following her. When she finally reached her destination, she pulled into the car park and sat for a while, head on the steering wheel, trying to collect her thoughts.

It's no use, she thought. *I'll just have to go up there tonight, talk it over.*

She sighed, exited and locked her car and began

the trek up the hill. She didn't see the car parked in darkness, and didn't recognise the sporty car that stopped to allow her to cross the road to the gate.

She was halfway up the hill when she heard it, a laboured breathing even louder than her own.

"Annabel!" The voice was harsh, dreadful. Her ex. Brandon.

"Are you following me?" She stopped and turned, angry that he was about to ruin her special place.

"You know it's not safe out here. I worry about you."

"You gave up the right to worry about me when we divorced." A slap in the face that glanced off, unfelt.

"I'll always worry about you."

"There's no need."

"I only ever wanted a happy marriage."

"You've got that, haven't you?"

"You know what I meant. With you."

"But you're not with me. You have her. Go home."

He was coming closer. He should have been going away.

"Not until I get what I came for."

"Leave me alone." She turned away and started climbing again. His hand on her shoulder stopped her.

"You need to listen to me."

"You need to let me go."

He spun her around, trapping her arm behind her back, claiming her lips. Harsh. Angry. Painful. She bit him. He yelped, tightened his grip on the arm he held behind her back and raised his other arm to slap her. She winced, eyes squeezed shut, waiting for the pain.

"The lady asked you to leave her alone!"

Her eyes flew open and she jerked her head towards the sound, accidentally clocking Brandon in the jaw. He cursed.

"Who do you think you are?"

"You're hurting my friend. I'd suggest you leave her alone. Now."

"Are you going to make me?"

"I won't have to." Roderick stared in amazement at the spectre coming towards them from the chapel on the hill.

"Do you think I was born yesterday? I'm not falling for that."

"What?"

"You. Looking behind me. As if there's something there."

"Suit yourself."

Roderick beckoned to the spectre. "He's all yours."

Brandon yelped again as a cold, metallic blade

rested on his exposed neck. He dropped Annabel's arm and slowly turned around. He could see nothing, but the feeling of the cold steel was still there. A warmth trickled down his neck. He wiped his hand across his neck and came away with blood. His.

"What the......!"

"I think you should leave."

"You'll pay for this! I'm calling the cops."

Roderick shrugged. "Be my guest." Brandon ran off in terror and the spectre disappeared.

Annabel turned towards the chapel on the hill.

"What was it? I saw nothing."

"It looked like a knight, but glowed?" Roderick shrugged again. "It doesn't matter. You're safe now."

"Did you follow me?"

"I just felt I had to."

"I'm, er, glad you did." Annabel looked down at her feet, and shivered as Roderick's hand lifted her chin. Their eyes met and once again, Annabel found herself swimming. Gently, Roderick claimed her, soothing away the pain, holding her close to his heart.

"I think I love you," she whispered.

"I know I love you," he whispered back.

"Come with me." She led him up to the ruined church. "This is my special place. I only invite special people here."

"Brandon?"

"Never invited. Must have followed me one day. I found this place when I needed to get away from him."

"Figures!"

****

Tallulah flew ahead, anxious now to join the party. Her work was done. Well, Prince Roderick hadn't asked Princess Annabel to marry him, but they'd both declared their love. It was as good as in the bag. She hoped she hadn't missed the coronation.

She glanced down at her woollen tunic and realised she was not dressed for a gala.

Is it too late to change? The moon had found a space in the fog and the pale silvery light illuminated the damp heather.

Perfect! She thought and with a liberal sprinkling of fairy dust, she had created a heather-purple gown of exquisite design. She borrowed some silvery moonlight and infused it with the drops of mist on a spider web to sprinkle on her hair and wings, then glided down to take her place at the gathering.

"Is it done?"

She turned to her inquisitor and nodded.

"Then where are they?"

"On their way up."

"Here? Is that wise?"

"Probably not, but this is her special place. It's where I expected her to come after tonight."

Lucas shrugged. "Guess it won't hurt. They'll not see us anyway."

"Have the festivities begun yet?" Tallulah hoped she hadn't missed anything.

"Just the preliminaries." He glanced at her. Curious ... "Guests of honour haven't arrived."

Tallulah raised a delicate eyebrow. "Really? I'm not late, then!"

***

Annabel held Roderick's hand and nearly dragged him up the hill. The night air was crisp and seemed charged with electricity. Up here, the mist had cleared and the stars twinkled. Roderick saw the isolated lights of the moor homes interspersed with the dark shapes of the moors and tors, glowing faintly through the misty moonlight.

"I've always loved the moors. These are different to those at my home, but there's still a magic to them. Best shown. Words just cannot describe."

Annabel smiled. She knew exactly what he meant. A gentle breeze ruffled her hair and she shivered.

"Cold? Let's see if it's warmer inside the ruin."

Roderick took her hand this time, and led her inside. The moonlight shone through the gaps in the ancient stonework, and filtered through the missing tiles of the roof. It was warmer inside, but still cold.

Their breath created a mist all its own, melding with the moonlight to create ethereal, silver threads that swirled around them.

"There must be some sort of mineral in these walls." Roderick took off his glasses to get a closer look at the tiny sparkling specks.

"Maybe." Annabel followed him to the wall, ducking under his arm to take advantage of his warmth. "I've seen this before, but not every night. Last time was probably about six months ago..."

"You come here often, then?" Roderick winced. It sounded like a lousy pick up line. If Annabel thought so, she didn't let on.

"Not so much nowadays. When Brandon and I were still together I think I was here more than at home."

"And yet, you're here tonight..."

She pursed her lips. "Yeah. It's my thinking place." She was quiet for a long time and Roderick thought she may actually want him to leave. She was still tucked under his arm and he was reluctant to make the suggestion.

She sighed.

"You'll think I'm mad, but... usually when I come up here, I just ... talk ... about... well... everything really. And then when I come away... well, somehow I can see better. Not ... physically, that would be daft. I just, well, you know ..."

He squeezed her shoulders.

"You're not daft ..."

He guided her to a ledge and they sat together, silently comfortable with each other's company. Annabel rested her head on his shoulder and he rested his chin on her head.

"You still smell gorgeous," he whispered.

****

Tallulah enjoyed the music and dancing. Lucas swirled her around, the sparkling silver drops of spider-web-dew left a faint trail. She was lucky to be here, but she was a little put out that the guests of honour still hadn't made their appearance.

"What's taking so long?" she asked.

Lucas smiled and spun her around again.

"Guests of honour keep to their own timetable," he said, giving her a saucy wink. She pouted, and made as if to fly away, but Lucas grabbed both her hands and flung her into a double roll, deftly flying after her, ready to catch her when she came out.

"Do you think I should check on Prince Roderick and Princess Annabel?"

"No need," said Lucas. "Look."

Tallulah looked.

****

"You know, you're nothing like..." Annabel felt the fire

suffuse her face, and she dropped the hand that she had been about to place on his knee into her own lap, gripping it with her other one.

Roderick chuckled.

"Has my ex-wife been telling tales?"

"Oh, well ... erm... She has said a thing or two. I prefer to make up my own mind, though... about ... people... you know?" She lapsed into silence, trying to take a deep, steadying breath without seeming to. What was it about him that affected her so?

He shifted a little on the bench and gently took her chin in his hand...

"Can I tell you a secret?" he asked, and she raised her eyes to look at him.

She wasn't sure exactly what it was she saw, but he suddenly looked different, somehow more intense, and yet ... powerfully gentle.

"Of course." He only knew she spoke because he saw her lips move.

She stared into his eyes, moonlight reflecting in hers, leaving him breathless. He sighed and felt the pull of the magic, drawing them closer together.

"Can you feel it? The magic of the Moors. It's all around us."

Annabel was silent, struggling to maintain her clarity, feeling herself drowning in his essence.

"I've never felt so strongly about anything before,

and I know we've never really been... well... out, but...
"

Roderick dropped to one knee, took her hand in his and said ...

"Will you marry me?"

****

The silence was deafening as the faerie folk held their collective breaths. All faces turned to face the mortal couple, the Princess Annabel staring into the eyes of the Prince Roderick as he knelt and offered her his heart.

Tallulah was particularly agitated, her heart beating so fast she thought it must surely be able to transcend the veil that separated their worlds.

Say Yes! *she silently pleaded, unconsciously gripping Lucas's hand so tight his hand felt numb.*

Slowly, as one, the faerie folk exhaled, gliding towards the couple, who seemed to be caught in a time trap.

****

Oblivious to their audience, Annabel's thoughts whirled, making her feel dizzy.

Am I mad? I'm actually contemplating this! What would Chrystal say? What would Charity say? Do I care? I felt something, but is it... love?

"Yes," she whispered, still drowning, but now surrendering to it.

****

"She said Yes!!" Tallulah squealed. Grabbing Lucas's hands, she spun him around.

Lucas laughed. "Slow down, Tallulah! You'll make us both dizzy!"

"I'm sorry ... but ... I did it!" She squealed again - quietly this time, and didn't go off in a mad spin, although the grin remained.

"You certainly did, Tallulah!" The bass voice brought her back to reality.

"Father!" She demurely curtsied. "I am so sorry. I didn't mean to bring them here, but ... "

He silenced her with his up-raised hand.

"Come ... "

Tallulah's hand slipped out of Lucas's as she followed the old faerie towards the dais above the ledge upon which our mortal hero and heroine sat as they pledged their love.

"Here, child. Sit"

He gestured to the golden throne, the seat of honour.

"But ... this is for ... "

"It's for you, silly. For us!" Lucas, who had quietly followed, took his place beside her.

"I don't understand."

"Of course you don't, child. I'm old. My time as King

is over, and with your mother having already ... Well, you know." He wiped a tear and straightened his back. "It's time."

****

Around them the ruined chapel exploded with light. Annabel and Roderick rose in amazement at the scene unfolding before their eyes. Tiny winged people flitted around what looked like a golden chandelier above their heads, lit by thousands of tiny candles. At the centre of the chandelier were two exquisite gold seats, thrones. And seated on these thrones were two tiny winged people, no taller than six inches each. Both were dressed in the colour of purple heather, the girl's dress sparking like tiny diamonds in the glow. Thousands of tiny creatures flitted about. Sweet music filled the air. Silk streamers caught the glow of both the moonlight and candlelight.

"Princess Annabel and Prince Roderick!" announced a curious little faerie, reading from a scroll, and a rather regal faerie man flew down to hover about a foot in front of them.

"We are honoured you have accepted our invitation."

"I ... I don't understand." Annabel shook her head, fascinated, and perhaps a little afraid of the scene before her. Roderick put a protective arm around her shoulder and gave her a reassuring squeeze.

"You come here often - maybe they think ..."

"Shh!" The regal faerie motioned for them to be seated again as a line of tiny trumpeters announced the start of the ceremony.

It was a surprisingly quiet ceremony - well, two ceremonies, actually. The first looked remarkably like a wedding. The little bride looked dazed, but certainly radiantly happy. The second was a coronation.

"That's my daughter!" The old faerie whispered, and Annabel thought she caught a glimpse of a diamond-like sparkle falling from his eye. He flitted away from them, up to the happy couple on the chandelier. He took his daughter's hand, touched his forehead to hers, and then ... disappeared. Her companion, now husband, copying Roderick's gesture, put his arm across her shoulders and drew him to her.

Annabel felt a surge of emotion for this tiny couple, but still had no idea why she was here. Before she could pluck up the courage to ask, the scene faded.

"Wait!"

The glow around the chandelier brightened again and Tallulah and Lucas floated down to hover where her father had been only moments before.

"I don't understand."

The faerie folk clasped their tiny hands over their rather pointed little ears, a flash of pain flitted across their faces.

"Sorry!" Annabel barely breathed the word and they nodded their appreciation at her consideration.

"I didn't understand either, at first, but now I do. My name is Tallulah. I have been your faerie guide since you started coming here..."

"You were real? I thought ... I was ... just speaking to my ... myself." Annabel's eyes, already brimming, spilled a single teardrop. Lucas looked horrified.

"You can't do that here! We'll drown!"

Annabel gulped and reigned in the tears.

"Sorry!"

"That's okay. We'd be able to contain the flood, although salt water isn't natural in these parts." Tallulah cast a furtive glance at Lucas. She continued, "We were so worried for you and I was given the task of helping you find true happiness. I followed you around a bit and noticed that Prince Roderick ... well, had feelings for you. I was given the deadline of tonight."

"Why tonight?"

"I can answer that." Lucas said. "Faerie folk have a King and a Queen - there has to be both. Tallulah's mother ... erm ... passed a year ago. The King therefore had a year to either find himself another Queen, or abdicate and name his successor. He has had many Queens over the years, and has many children. Tallulah is the youngest."

"Is it the youngest that ..."

"Oh, no!" Lucas laughed. "It is the most worthy. And that is Tallulah." He looked at his bride with such love, Annabel's heart ached a little more.

"But," said Tallulah, "the King can't just name his successor. He has to prove she, or he, is worthy. And so I was given this task. Of course, I thought ... Well, it doesn't matter what I thought. What matters is that I succeeded."

"Your father, the King. He disappeared," said Roderick. "Is he..."

"Dead? Heavens no! He's just gone to be with my mother."

"But..."

"Shh. We can't explain it. You wouldn't understand." Tallulah looked at a tiny watch on her wrist. "We need to re-join my people, but before we do..."

"You're going to take away our memories, aren't you?"

"Please don't," Annabel's plea tugged at Tallulah's heart.

"My hands are tied, but I can promise you this..."

****

"I think we should get you home," Roderick whispered into Annabel's ear. "You're chilled through."

It was true; she was shivering, but she didn't think

it was with the cold. Did she really agree to marry a man she barely knew? With some trepidation she looked up at Roderick, who still had his arm draped over her shoulders, lending his warmth, comforting her.

Yes she did. And in true fairy-tale fashion, they lived happily ever after.

.

A Moment in Time

I glanced at my watch, not for the first time, I might add, as I sat on the sofa, waiting.

"He's late," I muttered to no one in particular. "Not a good impression for a first date."

Just when I had almost given him up, a sharp rap on the door announced his arrival. Sally, my flatmate and best friend forever, galloped down the stairs to let him, announcing his arrival in her usual manner.

"Maggie! Your date's here!" she yelled, although the tiny flat certainly did not warrant such a noisy announcement. "She's through ..." I saw her point vaguely in my general direction and wandered back up the narrow staircase leading to the two tiny bedrooms and even tinier bathroom in what was essentially the roof space. My date poked his head through the arch opening that led to our multipurpose kitchen / diner / lounge area which took up the rest of the ground floor.

"Sorry I'm late," he said, and that was it. No explanation, just a breezy apology. I took in his fresh, just-graduated-from-high-school face sitting atop a slim, athletic body and shrugged. Guess I could do worse.

"No probs, Brad," I said. "Do you want a drink before we go, or should we just ..."

Why did I do this? I just wanted to get this date over and done with. I hope I hid my annoyance with a cheery smile. And I hope it didn't come across as a grimace.

"Nah. We should just get going. Don't want to miss ... erm ..." His voice trailed off, vanishing into the next thought and he motioned for me to accompany him to the door. My door, mind you. I don't think he noticed my thick, usually curly hair that Sally had kindly spent hours straightening, or my skin-tight jeans topped with a dainty, flowy top; my flawless make-up ... In fact, I doubt he even really looked at me at all! I sighed, glanced at Sally peaking at us from the top of the stairs, shooting daggers at her and followed him out to the red sports.

It was a lovely day out, the one day of summer, I'd say; a beautiful but incredibly rare sunny early English Summer's day. The top was down and I thought he'd raise it before we took off. He didn't. Normally, I'd have been thrilled to drive in a classy little sports car. If I'd known this was how we'd be travelling, I'd have been more prepared. I decided to see how it went, but after a very short ride, I couldn't stand being hair-whipped any longer so I gathered it all behind me and knotted it into a messy bun. It helped, a little. I had to hold the bun to keep it from unravelling, but at least with the top down there was really no opportunity for conversation. And for once, the radio was playing decent tunes.

****

Of all the luck! I arranged a date, the first with Maggie, this babe I met online and, wouldn't you know it, Argyle are in the semis. I thought I should probably cancel the date and watch the game instead, but then I remembered just how gorgeous she was, and I didn't think she'd appreciate that. I really haven't been out with a chick this gorgeous since ... Well, let's just say it's been a while. I decided to go, and told myself I could watch the game on my iPhone, during the date.

Well, it seemed like a good idea at the time.

I was just a little late picking her up, but she looked at me like I was hours late. Come to think of it, I may have been a half hour late. There's really no excuse considering it turns out I actually live very close (amazing that we hadn't bumped into each other before this), but the match started and I just thought I'd pick her up during half time, and I figured we could just about make it there during the ads before the next half. Well, sticking to times isn't really my strong suit. She actually offered me a drink before we went, but I was sticking to a schedule - I needed to get to the castle before half-time started - or at the very least, before the game was over.

I picked her up in an MG Roadster I'd borrowed for the date. You know, got to impress the lady! She looked gorgeous, even better than her profile picture, which in itself is amazing because, in my vast experience, the girls never look as good as their pics. There's an exception to every rule!

Anyway, the weather was perfect - so hot. Our one day of summer had decided to arrive today. To celebrate, I decided we'd travel with the top down. If any of my mates saw me, I wanted them to be sure to see this beauty I'd picked up. Conversation was going to be difficult, so I tuned in to Heart Radio and just let the radio do the talking. I don't think she minded the radio, but I did notice we hadn't gone very far when she'd grabbed all that gorgeous hair and twisted it into a messy knot at the back of her head. And she kept holding it, as if it was going to blow away. She looked rather like one of my teachers at school - NOT my favourite, and I was a little put off by that. Still, I had made the effort to come on this date, and I was going to put any negative thoughts behind me. Enjoy the day. I did wish she'd just let her hair fly, though. Or maybe she could have worn a pretty scarf. Never mind.

***

It was mid-afternoon by the time we arrived at the ruined Berry Pomeroy castle we'd chosen as a neutral spot for our first date. This is a magical castle, hidden from view by the forest in which it was built. I jumped out of the car, released my hair from the ridiculous bun and combed my fingers through it, gently pulling out the knots, hoping to restore some order. I must have looked a sight – some lad out with his lady gave me a weird look and I caught the tail end of a malicious stare from her. I lowered my gaze, a little bit annoyed that she'd been so hostile. I really didn't set out to attract anyone – except perhaps Brad. He, though, was oblivious.

Brad grabbed my hand and almost dragged me into the ruin. I stopped to read the first of the information boards dotted in strategic places around the site. Brad dropped my hand and walked on ahead.

"Let's see if we can get some signal," he murmured. His phone had become attached to his hands and his eyes glued to the screen from the moment he had stepped inside the crumbling stone walls. He looked behind and saw me still standing there.

"You coming?" he asked, gesturing for me to join him in what I assumed he thought was a 'come hither' look. I'd finished reading the sign, so, with a reluctant sigh I followed him to a park bench in a secluded spot with a view. We sat together in what I can only describe as awkward silence. Brad checked his phone while I sat with my hands clasped demurely in my lap, tapping my feet.

"Erm ... Shall we ... have a look around?" I just needed to move. The park bench was hard and already my butt was going numb.

"Hmm ... sure," Brad answered. "I'll just ...Woah, get in there!"

I glanced over at his phone to see ridiculously tiny men kicking a ball, a ball so small it was merely a white fleck on the screen.

Football! I shook my head and sat a while longer, waiting for him to pay me some attention. I wondered, not for the first time today, how I'd agreed to this date. Sure, he looked like his e-Harmony profile, but where was the adventure-loving romantic he had described? Certainly not sitting here beside me right now!

"What do you think this was?" I asked, waving my arms about to encompass the grassed area immediately around the park bench we were sitting on. It was a rough rectangle, delineated by whitened rock embedded into the ground. The walls of the castle were a good five or ten metres away. "I wonder if it was a small courtyard for the ladies to sun themselves. What do you think?" I prodded him with my make-believe parasol, waving a make-believe fan in front of my face to coquettishly cool my face.

"Huh? Oh, yeah ... probably."

"I'm just going to ..." I sighed and stood, stretching my now comatose butt. I wandered off towards another of the information boards. When I got there, I looked back. Brad, still engrossed in the football match, didn't seem to notice I was gone.

Some date this is turning out to be! I thought, and

mentally kicked myself for breaking my own rule about dating sites. If I was being perfectly honest, at the not-so-tender age of 25, I was beginning to despair of finding the man of my dreams within my limited social circle. Sally had met a wonderful man online, and had encouraged me to give it a go. I will never, ever, not in a million years, put myself through this again! I left Brad to his football and went exploring.

I rounded the corner and stepped into a gloriously fragrant garden filled with roses, lavender, chrysanthemums, peonies and daisies. Apple blossoms added their scent from a couple of trees strategically placed and surrounded by the colourful blossoms. A cobbled path led to a delightful well and I resisted the urge to toss a few coins in for good luck.

I stood for a minute, breathing in the warm, heady fragrance. The soft green lawn beckoned and I kicked off my pumps, letting my toes sink into the luxuriance. I bent to collect my shoes and rose to stand face-to-face with a young girl dressed in a simple black dress and frilly white apron. On her head was a white cotton mop cap and she carried a small tray, laden with the makings of a delicate afternoon tea for one.

"Where will you be wanting your tea, Lady Margaret?" she said.

"I ... erm ... that is to say ... erm ..."

I'm a naturally shy person, so stumbling over my words isn't new to me. The young girl was looking straight at me so I assumed it was me she was addressing, but I haven't been called Margaret for, well, forever. I know it's my name - I've seen my birth certificate - but even when I was naughty as a child, and let's face it, we all are at some stage, I was always called "Mags", or "Maggie", or even "Maggot" by some particularly nasty girls at school, but never "Margaret". And most certainly never "Lady" anything! I was about to say this, but suddenly found my arm in a vice-like grip by an elegant but evidently angry woman. She was dressed in a flowing gown, low-waisted, and pulled in tight across her bust and waist, flowing over her hips, the skirt open to reveal an intricately embroidered underskirt in muted complementary colours. Her dress was delicate and feminine, but her demeanour was not.

"She'll take her tea in the tower. Run along," she snapped at the poor girl, who executed a perfect curtsy without so much as a clink of china or silverware.

"Yes, Lady Eleanor," she murmured and scuttled off in the direction of the tower to the right forming a corner of the castle wall immediately beside the main house.

I was impressed with her agility, but felt a little sorry for her, being the brunt of the "Lady Eleanor's" ire, but I soon came to believe she had it lucky, compared to me.

"Come, my dear. You know it's not good for you to be outside on a day like this."

I thought this was a bit of play-acting taken to the extreme, and so I followed the older woman through the courtyard, which, to be honest, looked old, yet not as old as the outside of the castle had seemed when we first arrived. I was also surprised to see that, around the corner from where Brad and I had been sitting, there didn't appear to be a ruin at all. The garden I have already described, but the house! It was clearly habitable. Indeed, judging by the open windows with drapes wafting in the breeze, very comfortably so. The house appeared to be of a smooth cream stone, possibly a type of concrete covering the grey stone that the house must have been made from, if the ruin I had seen earlier was any indication.

We didn't go to the front entrance, although I tried to move in that direction. Lady Eleanor's grip on my arm tightened, if it was at all possible, and I found myself being almost dragged away from the sounds of pleasant chatter and the clinking of china coming from the open windows of what may have been a parlour. Light piano music was playing – a real party which I was obviously not going to be attending.

"This is all very ... interesting ... but I really have to get back to my date ..." I felt my skin turn to ice as my companion, or rather, captor, turned her gaze on me. She looked angry, and I couldn't for the life of me understand why.

"I, I'm sorry," I stammered. "Do I know you? Where are we going?" The Lady Eleanor shot me another scathing sideways look, lip curling in disgust.

"Really, Margaret. I tire of your games," and she yanked on my already aching arm, forcing me to continue to stroll alongside her. "And why on earth are you wearing your underwear outside?"

I looked down at my blue jeans and floaty peasant-style top, then back at her elaborate garb and shrugged. Really, what could I say? Clearly this was not underwear I was wearing. I began to feel my companion might be insane, and so made the judicious decision to play along, for the moment. She dragged me over to the heavy wooden door that marked the entry to the Tower, opened the door and pushed me inside.

It was dark inside, at least, much darker than the brilliant sunshine of the garden. When my eyes adjusted, it was to see a spiral staircase leading upwards. Otherwise, the room was bare, the only light being provided by the open door behind me and a thin opening at the foot of the stairs. Lady Eleanor pushed me towards the stairs.

"Up you go," she said. There seemed to be nothing I could do but obey. Two hundred painful, stifling, claustrophobic steps later I found myself in a small circular room. I'm exaggerating. I'm sure it wasn't two hundred steps but it certainly felt like it. This circular room was furnished.

A small canopied bed occupied a space between two tiny slits of windows and by another, a small table with a solitary chair was positioned. A small alcove on one 'side' of the circle, hidden from open sight by a heavy curtain, revealed what I could only assume was a latrine, a stone bench with a chute leading down. And the stench was counteracted somewhat by the sprigs of dried lavender, rosemary, rose petals and other herbs hanging from yet another slit of a window space. I think the heavy curtain was supposed to block some of the smell as well, and I'm sure it tried.

Opposite the latrine was a small dresser on top of which was a small freestanding mirror of polished metal, a rudimentary brush and comb set, and a pitcher and bowl. And beside that was a tri-fold screen, over which was draped a few beautiful dresses, similar to the one worn by the Lady Eleanor.

I thought Lady Eleanor had followed me up but she hadn't, and so I thought I might as well have a bit of a rest before making my way back down. I sat on the solitary chair at the table by the window, looking out over the courtyard, or what I could see of it. A soft voice roused me from my introspection, and I saw the same maid from before.

"Your tea, M'Lady," she said, laying out the makings and then pouring a dainty drop into a piece of fine bone china. I thanked her, and, lifting the cup to my lips, blew gently on the hot liquid. The fragrant infusion pleased my nostrils and I took a tentative sip. It was still too hot and I grimaced. Something about the maid's manner caught my attention and I froze, the cup poised for a further sip.

"Is there something wrong?" I asked.

"N...No, M'Lady," she stammered, then gently took my cup from my hand and poured a bit of tea into the saucer. She then handed me the saucer. I frowned a little, but the sad look on her face suggested I may have done something wrong after all. I took the saucer and after testing the temperature with my lip, had a small sip. My actions were rewarded with a relieved smile.

"Will there be anything else, M'Lady?" she asked.

I smiled and shook my head, not really knowing what else to do. She curtsied and turned to go, then turned back to me and said, "We all hope you get well soon, M'Lady." She then curtsied again and fled down the stairs.

The tea had left an odd taste in my mouth, so I made an executive decision not to have any more of it. There was no sound in the tower. I assumed either the sound of the door closing was simply not audible from here, or the maid knew another way. This was all so strange. I had no idea what was going on and I had no intention of finishing this tea. Seeing as Lady Eleanor hadn't followed me upstairs I decided it was time to leave. I looked at my watch and was surprised to see only ten minutes had passed since I was sitting beside Brad, bored out of my skull, wishing I was anywhere but here. Funny thing is I still wished I wasn't here, but I found myself beginning to yearn for the company of the football-mad boy I had met on the internet.

***

Well, we lost the game and I turned to Maggie to finally get this date started. She wasn't there. I assumed she'd gone for a wander and if I was being perfectly honest, I would have done the same. Let's face it. I was not a good date.

I wandered about the ruins, but could find no sign of her. Berry Pomeroy is simply a ruined wall enclosing an old castle, of which not much remains and a crumbling mansion. Only at the entrance through the portcullis and to the right was there any complete rooms, and I had been in them, including the old keep, which was essentially a mini museum.

Outside the complex, English Heritage, who oversaw many of England's ruins, had built a gift shop and tearooms, so I thought she may have wandered over there. She hadn't. She also hadn't wandered by the gate that led to the field where two gorgeous shire horses grazed, and she wasn't in the women's conveniences. I know this because I waited outside them for an uncomfortably long time.

By this time, I will admit to feeling a little annoyed with her. How dare she just wander off without telling me where she was going? I even thought she may have gone off with someone else, although it was only other couples and families who had come here, and, from what I could see, I was the only single person there. Maggie wasn't there. Perhaps she'd called for a taxi!

I wandered back down to the car park, thinking she may have given up waiting for me inside and decided to wait in the car. It was a convertible and I'd not bothered putting the canopy up. You don't need to unless it's raining. No one can steal it!

The car was empty.

I noticed a leggy blonde watching me as she walked back to her car with her companion. They both looked vaguely familiar and I wondered if perhaps they'd seen us. I asked.

"Don't tell me you've misplaced that ... bimbo you were with?" The leggy blonde sneered. Her companion shot her a puzzled look. He turned back to me.

"I remember. You arrived the same time we did. I haven't seen your lady friend since. Sorry." He shook his head at the leggy blonde and led her to their car. I wasn't sure what all that was about. I doubted they actually knew Maggie, and I certainly had never seen them before today. At any rate, this wasn't helping me find her.

I thought perhaps she may have decided to go for a walk in the woods around the castle, but remembering her footwear, I doubted it. I did wander a short way along the trail, but the recent rain had rendered the path pretty much impassable, and after only a very short distance, I could see no one had ventured down there today.

It was nearly closing time and now I was beginning to panic. I had her mobile number of course, and dialled the number before realising I had no signal. If I had no signal, I could bet she didn't either.

There was nothing for it. I would have to go back inside the ruin and look again. She had to be there somewhere.

***

I don't know how long I sat at the small table with my cold tea on the tray in front of me. I couldn't bring myself to drink it, and I admit to being a tad confused and just a little wary of this role playing scenario I seemed to have become roped into.

Eventually, I made my way downstairs, thinking I'd like to take another turn in the garden, but was surprised to find that the garden door was locked. As the only other opening on the ground floor was the slit in the blocks for a window, I understood I was never going to get out that way, at least until this role play was over. The light coming in through the slit was not very bright, and the room itself was rather small, but I still hoped I'd find a way out. I ran my hands along the wall. Perhaps there would be a secret door leading to another part of the castle and from which I could make my escape. I could feel nothing.

I didn't relish the walk back up those stairs, but I also didn't fancy being in the dark for so long and so I slowly made my way up, feeling along the walls of the spiral staircase, hoping for another way out. I did find a very narrow door, also locked about a quarter of the way up, and then another a few more turns around the spiral. This one was shut, but my tentative efforts revealed that it could indeed be opened.

My elation was short-lived. It may have led to the

main house, but at the end of a very short corridor was another door. And this one was locked. It did have the advantage of what passed for a window, however, but although it was slightly wider than the ones on the ground floor, it was still impassable to me.

I returned to the staircase and my upward journey. At what I estimated to be a few spirals short of what I had now come to think of as 'my' tower room, I came to another door. This one was obviously not locked as it was indeed ajar. I had missed it on my way down, but to be fair, I wasn't looking at the time, intent as I was on regaining access to the garden.

I stepped through this door, and found myself to be on what I believe may have once been termed a 'widow's walk', simply a passageway around the roof of a house. There was a low block wall – about waist height, and I leaned against this wall, straining a little to see the ground below, wondering if this was how I could make my escape.

The ground was too far below.

I sighed and turned my back on the glorious view of Devon forest with barely a habitation in view. I was trapped. I knew it. What I didn't know was how. Or even why. One minute I had been enjoying a stroll in the garden, trying to make the best of what had turned out to be a bit of a fizzle of a date, and the next... well, you know my story. 'Lady Margaret'! Well, I'd rather be just plain 'Maggie' and right now I'd give anything to be home safe and well.

"There you are!"

My heart leapt to my throat at the harsh exclamation from the Lady Eleanor.

"I was bored and wanted to take a stroll. The garden door seems to be locked so I came up here."

"You didn't have your tea," she said, ignoring my comment about the locked door.

"I wasn't thirsty."

I turned back to the view.

"Why am I here?"

I don't know if I expected an answer, but I certainly wanted one. As dates go, this was the strangest one I'd been on. I'd long gotten over my pique of sentimentality in wishing he was with me. I guess I was angry with him, blaming him for my being in this predicament. I never once thought he had actually wished me harm. It was just that his lack of attention had led to my wandering off on my own, and that had led to this. I had thought I was a 'prisoner' in some weird role play, but it had slowly dawned on me that I wasn't just in a physical prison, and this was probably not a role play.

I knew enough about Berry Pomeroy Castle to know that there was only one area of the ruin that was anywhere close to being intact. And I was not in it.

I had a vague recollection of this ruin being haunted and I wondered if I had somehow managed to cross into another plane of existence. My rational mind told me not to be stupid, that this was an impossible fantasy, and not a good one at that. But my experiences! How else could I explain the serving girl, the haughty Lady Eleanor, the costuming? At first I had thought it was playacting, so that could explain all of that. But nothing in my experience could possibly explain the fact that I was now inside a fully-functional tower attached to a mansion that should have been just a shell.

I felt Lady Eleanor move closer to me. All my senses were now alert. It was no surprise that I didn't trust her.

"Because, my dear sister," and she spat out the words, leaving me in no doubt that the poor Lady Margaret was not liked by her sister at all, "you have caught the eye of the man I am going to marry."

"But I ..."

She grabbed my hair and dragged me to the other side of the roof along walk.

"There! See how he looks for you, even now!"

I peered down at the garden below and by some trick of the light I could see the garden as it once was, superimposed on the garden as it now is – just plain grass with ruined walls. I could see two men of similar build, one wearing stocking and breeches with a long coat and a tri-cornered hat, the other in faded blue denim jeans and a checked shirt, hatless with his spiky blond hair.

"Brad!" I screamed his name and for my troubles, had my hair yanked and I was dragged back towards the roof/tower access. I hoped, but couldn't be sure, that he had heard me.

Lady Eleanor pushed me inside and I struggled to retain my footing, the spiral staircase being literally just inside the door. She let go of my hair in order to close and lock the door. What happened next I can only blame on my disorientation. I ran up the stairs!

Why did I not run down? I know the garden door was locked, but surely down would have been the obvious choice? Nevertheless, it was up that I went.

I made it to the tower room where I had been served my tea, but, what I hadn't noticed before is that the staircase continued to climb. My room was not at the end of the staircase. I made a snap decision to climb higher.

The staircase opened out to the roof. Above me now was just air and around me was the crenelated wall of the top of the tower. I had nowhere to go. Despite the ridiculous gown she was wearing, and therefore the slowness of her climb, the Lady Eleanor now had me more trapped than if I'd stayed put in my tower prison.

I don't know why I did it, or what I'd hoped to gain, but when I saw the Lady Eleanor emerge on the tower roof, I climbed onto the wall. I don't do heights at the best of times and with the Lady Eleanor behind me, I didn't really feel my life was going to be prolonged. She had murderous intent, and for all intents and purposes, I had just played into her hands.

I closed my eyes, mainly to block out the dizzying height, and, helped by the Lady Eleanor, I slowly toppled forward.

***

It was only a few minutes to closing time now, and I knew I couldn't stay here much longer. I had no idea what I was going to do, and had even contemplated hiding in the dungeon at the bottom of the ruined tower until the workers had locked up for the night. I kept thinking she must have been playing a game with me, hiding when she saw me, and then changing her hiding place when my back was turned. But, apart from the blocked off areas, and a padlocked, grated well, there were not really any good places she could have done that.

I had retraced my steps to the bench where I'd spent most of my time, and then took off in what I thought was the most logical place she could have gone to explore the ruins. I remembered her question, only vaguely, seeing as my attention was elsewhere, about what I thought the garden might have been used for back in the day, and then, she took off towards the house.

I followed that thought and just stood in the centre of what must have once been a magnificent garden for the ladies to take a walk in, slowly turning around, looking at the ruined walls around me.

And then I swear I heard her call my name.

It seemed like it was coming from above me. I looked up at the ruined tower, but could see no one there. There wasn't really any way of getting up there – not safely anyway, and yet, I just couldn't shake the feeling that she was there. I slowly walked towards the tower, straining to see, straining to hear. Nothing. I tried to climb the wall, but, even though there were quite a few good hand and foot holds, it just wasn't enough, and the moss and lichen on the walls made it slippery.

I was about to give up and just report her as missing.

I looked up again, and just for a moment, I swear I saw the whole tower, smooth stone walls, heavy wooden doors, embrasures strategically placed for the archers, and a crenelated wall at the very top. And on top of that wall, I saw her.

"Maggie!" I screamed her name and the stragglers turned to look.

"What the ..."

"Who's ..."

"How did she get ..."

Pandemonium!

I watched, helpless, as the figure began to free-fall, gracefully diving from the top of Lady Margaret's Tower.

"Oh my God!" I didn't know what to do, so I just

stood there, my arms outstretched, ready to catch her, staring as she fell. What was I thinking? Someone falling from that height would crush the person they fell on!

The body fell into my arms and I felt ... nothing.

"It's Lady Margaret!" One of the guides rushed over to me. "She falls from this tower just about every evening at this time, reliving her death at the hand of her sister."

"But ...?" I stared at the guide and then at my empty arms, dumfounded. "Maggie ..."

I heard a moan from just inside the tower ruin.

"It's just the ghost."

I wasn't convinced.

"Maggie?" I entered the darkened doorway, not sure what I'd find there.

"Brad?"

It was barely a whisper.

"What ... How ... Are you okay?"

"I ... fell."

"Are you hurt? Can you stand?" I reached down to help her up. She was clearly stunned, but didn't appear to be badly damaged. Still I thought it best to hold her up and so put my arm around her waist. I was surprised when she leant into me, but assumed she found she was hurt more than she thought.

The guide wanted to check her out for any serious injuries and call an ambulance. I was happy to do this, but Maggie said she just wanted me to take her home. I couldn't argue, and so, leaving her in the care of the guide, I brought the car up to the entrance. We both helped her into the car; I popped the canopy up as the evening had turned a little chilly and carefully drove her back.

***

I don't remember much about how I finally got home. I do remember falling ... and landing, although not as hard as I would have expected from the top of the tower. I also remember, although I know this bit isn't true, that Brad caught me when I fell. I know this isn't true because I then had a memory of Brad calling my name, and finding me at the base of the tower. I remember he helped me up and I had to lean on him for support. And it's funny how memories go because I actually remember that I felt safe in his arms.

I definitely don't remember the ride home, nor do I remember how I got up the stairs and into my flat. I do remember Sally's horrified face as she saw the state I was in when Brad returned me. I have a vague recollection of her yelling at him, and me, weakly, telling her to shut up, that this man had saved me and of Sally then standing with her mouth open in awe.

I have no recollection of climbing the stairs, of showering (although I woke up clean, so must have done) or of falling into bed.

I do remember waking up in a panic, my heart

racing and my head spinning, and a cool hand being placed on my forehead, whispered words of reassurance, me falling back to sleep.

I also remember waking to bright sunshine and realising I had slept all day and it was the afternoon sun waking me. And I remember seeing Brad, still in the same clothes he had been wearing the day before, gently snoring on one of our kitchen chairs that had miraculously appeared in my room.

"Brad?" He heard my whisper and jerked awake.

"Maggie, I'm so sorry ..."

"Shh ..." I reached for his hand which he put in mine. "Thank you. I thought she was going to kill me."

He gave me an odd look then, but I didn't care. I'd tell him all about it one day, but for now it was enough to know he had saved me. I closed my eyes and pretended to go back to sleep. I don't know for sure, of course, but I have a feeling Brad's the one.

***

I was surprised she didn't tell me to get out when she woke up and found me in her room. She thanked me for saving her life! I will spend the rest of my days making it up to her for neglecting her in the first place. I have a feeling I'll have all the time I need.

A Time to Heal

I remember as if it were yesterday, the day my daughter almost died.

I dragged myself from sleep as I became aware of a light tapping at my bedroom door. Glancing at the alarm clock on my side table, I squinted to see the bright red numbers. My eyesight is bad at the best of times. Still groggy from being awoken from sleep, I could only just make out the time. 2:30 am. Not too late after all, considering.

"Mum, I'm home"

"Thanks for letting me know, sweetheart. Did you have a good time?" I know my words slurred softly as I struggled to regain full consciousness.

My daughter hesitated, still standing in the doorway.

"Hmm," she said eventually, and turned to go to her own room and then off to bed.

I couldn't make out her features in the dim light, particularly as she was a silhouette with the hall light behind her, but something about her stance alerted me that all was not well. I sat up, prepared to follow her into her room. I didn't need to.

She sighed and crept into my room, perching on the edge of my bed.

"There was a bombing at the concert."

Her words, distorted by the ringing in my ears, came to me as if from a time tunnel and I wondered if I had heard her correctly.

"What?" I asked, acid rising from the pit of my stomach, burning. I breathed hard, fighting it down.

"I'm okay," she said. "We couldn't get home for a while, though. That's why I'm late. The train station was closed."

"What happened? How ..." I drew my daughter close. I'm mum. I had to control the panic and fear I was feeling. I knew it was irrational. My daughter was obviously safe, and yet the feeling of dread clenched my heart. It was a close call. Too close.

"We thought it was balloons at first. Ariana had let down a heap of huge balloons during the last song and one of them had popped. It was so loud and so when it went off, that's what we all thought it was."

Jen sat with her head down, hands covering her

mouth, breathing deeply. I don't remember having to teach her how to deal with panic. She was a first aider. I guess she was using the techniques on herself. I didn't really know how to comfort her, but my gut instinct was to just hold her and let her talk.

"Anyway, when we realised it was a bomb, everyone else had the same thought. I can't remember hearing anything else, really. Just some snatched conversations here and there as me, Niki, and Lou dragged each other out of the stadium, shouting to each other: we have to stick together. We couldn't go out the way we wanted to –the exit that led to Victoria. That's where the bomb was."

She stopped talking for a while then and looked at me. I could just make out her glittering eyes in the dimness of the room, reflecting the light from the mirror which in turn reflected light from the hallway.

"There was this smell of burned rubber ... Well, it was sort of like burned rubber."

"Oh," I said. I knew what she was describing and, although there may have been rubber in the carpet tiles of the stadium's foyer, what she was describing wasn't rubber. I hoped she'd never have to smell it again, but knew I had to let her know. Chances are she would smell burned rubber again and know that this was not what she had smelled that night.

"That may have been ... hair ... or ...," I stopped, took a deep breath and continued, "you know when you put your arm too close to the flame on the cooker ...?" My voice trailed off again as I watched the penny drop.

"Oh!" She sighed a deep, shuddering sigh. "I'll never forget that smell."

I nodded and stroked her hair as she continued her story.

"We couldn't get the train back, at least, not from Victoria, so we decided to walk to Piccadilly. We asked how far it was, but no one really knew and a security guard just pointed in the general direction. We walked for ages and didn't find it."

"Why didn't you call me? I could have come and picked you all up. You know I would have. I had my phone with me in case you did." It was the first time I had agreed to just go to bed when she went out, to not wait up.

I'm 18, Mum, she had said many times before and I always told her I just liked to make sure she was home before going to bed – it helped me sleep. She would roll her eyes and shake her head. I can take care of myself! I knew she was right - and this time, as she had walked out the door, I'd asked her if she had her key. She patted her purse, nodded, blew me a kiss and left the house. Now, I held my shaking daughter, stroking her hair, revelling in her relative safety, kicking myself for sleeping during her trauma.

"Lou had already phoned her brother to come and pick us up and he was on his way." Jen drew in a deep, shuddering breath.

"We came across an Ibis hotel and asked the lady

on the desk if we could just hang out here until Dan and his girlfriend came to pick us up. They were all so lovely. They knew we were at the concert – I guess our faces must have given it away. I think by now our make-up was all streaming down our faces. They gave us something to eat and drink and offered us a room at a discount price. Dan was already on his way so we declined."

She was silent again, eyes closed, fighting to maintain control.

"I'm so tired!"

I was going to ask her if she just wanted to go to sleep but didn't want her to think I didn't want her to talk. By now my sleepiness had pretty much gone. I continued to hold her close, vowing I would never let her go again, knowing it was a vow I shouldn't keep. She snuggled into me, perhaps vowing she would never go to a concert again. This vow she also shouldn't keep!

She sighed, sniffed and wiped her eyes, clearly having shed more silent tears.

"The hotel was playing the coverage of the news. It was horrible. I thought you might have seen it, and so I sent you a text."

"I never got it," I said, reaching for my phone. It still hadn't arrived. No doubt it would eventually, when it was too late to matter. I had gone to bed anyway, and so missed any news coverage I might have seen on Facebook. I was spared that.

"It doesn't matter now anyway."

"No. You're right. You're home safe, and that's what matters," I murmured into her hair. I could feel her relaxing against me, and then she stiffened.

"Mum, there were kids there," she blurted it out. "We were chatting with them as we were all waiting to go in, so excited, some going to their very first concert. They were so little. Some of them are probably dead." She sobbed then, quiet, heart-wrenching sobs. "It could have been me. It should have been me."

"Oh, baby girl. Shh ..." I held her closer, if it was at all possible, gently rocking her, soothing her as I had done all those years ago. "Shall I make you a cuppa?"

"Yes, please, with lots of honey." Jen dried her eyes, sniffed inelegantly and rose. I threw on a dressing gown and together we went down to the kitchen.

With super-sweet peppermint tea in hand, we sat on the sofa. Jen leant on me, soaking up the warmth and comfort that only a mother's hug can give. At least, I hope that's how she felt. I know I was enjoying the contact, knowing I had my daughter safe, and knowing that tonight, some mothers were not so lucky.

"Can we watch a movie?" she asked.

"Of course. Which one?"

"Tangled." It was an obvious choice – no thought

involved. It was Jen's favourite feel-good movie.

We put it on and silently watched for a moment.

"You know, I was so excited, when I left the house yesterday afternoon. I was looking forward to this concert for ages."

"I know," I said, stroking her lovely curls. She sighed.

"She's my idol – one of them, anyway," she continued. "You know I have many. She's so outspoken about women's rights, and her music is great. I just love her to bits."

I confess to not really having heard of her before Jen told me her friend, Niki, had invited her along. I would make a conscious effort to find out about her now, though, to see why someone would target her concert, to try to make some sense of an otherwise senseless act.

"I did feel a little uneasy when I was getting on the bus to the train station, more than I usually do taking public transport alone."

"I usually have the premonitions," I said, "Nothing this time, though. Perhaps I was too preoccupied with finally letting you let yourself in afterwards, not waiting up for you."

"Yeah, I know. You know, maybe it was a premonition of some sort after all, but I didn't feel I shouldn't go – It was just that I was uneasy about getting on the bus."

We sat in silence for a bit longer, focussing on the movie, but not really taking it in. We had seen it so many times before and could pretty much recite the dialogue. Jen could, anyway. I think she just wanted a sense of normality after the events of the evening.

She sighed. "We were laughing and joking – you know, just what friends do. We got there way early so we just hung out, chatting with the people in the crowd. We had seats so we weren't too worried about having to be at the front of the queue. We chatted with this lovely man who was raising awareness for WWF and he said there were jobs going with the organisation. I'd like to do something like this and he said I'd be good at it. He's based in Manchester, though. Anyway, he was really lovely. His stand would have been near the bomb blast."

Jen stopped talking, sipped her tea, fighting to keep it together. "I'm never going to a concert again."

I smiled then. She couldn't see me, but may have felt my facial muscles move. She didn't say anything, though. I did.

"I know you feel like that now. And perhaps you won't for a while. But you will one day."

She thought for a bit. "Maybe," she said. "Not at Manchester, though."

"Perhaps not." I agreed. It was too soon to let her know that she would get over this, after a fashion. Perhaps she would always be a little more cautious. Maybe even more wary of people in general, but I knew this wouldn't change her naturally caring nature. I knew this wouldn't cause her to hate a group of people for the acts of a few. She was made of stronger stuff and I know I'm right about this.

Eventually she said she was now so tired and just wanted to sleep. I gave her another hug and suggested that I'd seek the advice of a colleague in the morning, just to make sure we were handling this okay. I was sure we were.

Carry on as normal was the advice I was given, and that's exactly what we did.

The next day we traipsed off to Starbucks to write or draw. Her friends came over the next evening for a debrief with hot chocolate, chocolate cake and other treats. I don't know how much debriefing went on, but I did hear a lot of giggles, and on the weekend we went to The Shambles in York for a family outing. They were the sorts of things we would have done anyway. She did have the opportunity to go to the benefit concert the week after, but chose not to. She said it was too soon.

Not a lot of time has passed since the event, but the passage of time does heal. I don't think Jen's entirely over the ordeal. She is working through it, though. She's booked her next concert with the same friends and is looking forward to it. Life is looking up and she's positive about the future.

As for me, well, I'm getting over it, too. She's still my baby, but I've come to see in her the strong mature woman she has become. She'll eventually leave home and then I'll have different worries. Until then, every moment I have with her is precious.

My girl survived.

Blood Ties

"It has to be perfect!" Liv muttered, flitting around the room, tweaking a cushion here, flicking some imaginary dust off the coffee table, rearranging the already perfect arrangement of burgundy roses and seasonal foliage and ensuring the coasters lined up perfectly with each other. She then smoothed her linen skirt, ironing out imaginary wrinkles.

"She's always so picky." Liv sighed and glanced at the clock. "Not long now. Just enough time to straighten things up a little."

She went over the room again, rearranging things, adjusting the paintings, ensuring everything was lined up in perfect symmetry. It wasn't just for her stepmother's benefit. Liv needed order in her life, always had.

The hall mirror revealed her perfect make-up and

she pushed a small strand of hair back in place. Liv turned her body, checking that everything about her clothes, posture and style was perfect. It was.

"I think I'm done here."

A satisfied grin played about her lips and she looked at the clock again, knowing she still had a few more minutes before her stepmother, Judy, graced her with her presence. She wandered into the kitchen to put the finishing touches on the morning tea she would serve and had just finished arranging the tiny cakes and sandwiches on the trolley along with the silver urn of boiling water and selection of herb teas, including her stepmother's favourites, when the doorbell rang.

Not one to stand on ceremony, her guest entered the house.

"I'm here, Livvie, Darling!" she called.

Liv closed her eyes and took a deep breath.

"Make yourself at home, Mamma!" She wheeled the trolley to the living room and came to an abrupt halt. Her stepmother, white glove poised above the window ledge, ignored the clatter of crockery and continued her inspection. The stranger in the room greeted Liz with chocolate covered hand prints across the plush white carpet and a wide smile.

"Who's this?" she asked, resisting the urge to take out the Wet'n'Dry Vac to tackle the chocolate hand prints.

"Jackie, meet Livvie."

"How do you do, Jackie," said Liv. Seizing a napkin off the trolley and carefully extricating the toddler from the coffee table, she proceeded to wipe what was left of the chocolate from between his fingers.

"I wouldn't worry about that, dear." Judy inspected the glove and picked at an imaginary spot of dirt. "It's nothing compared to the state of these window ledges."

Liv held Jackie at arm's length and carried him into the kitchen.

"So whose is he, then?" she asked Judy, who had followed her. She ran the tap to warm and deposited Jackie on the bench. Jackie promptly splashed his hands in the running water, gurgling with delight. A few minutes later and his hands showed no trace of the chocolate, but Liv's worktop now sported a flood. It was beginning to drip onto the floor.

Judy gestured vaguely, looking at the now messy kitchen, tutting and shaking her head in disapproval.

"You really should clean up a bit better, Livvie, Darling," she said.

"So. Jackie?" Liv asked, picking the toddler up and dumping him unceremoniously in her stepmother's arms. "Whose child?"

She succumbed to the urge to mop up the spilled water on the worktop and dropped a load of paper towels onto the floor, dropping down herself to mop up the spill.

"Oh, you know …" she said, turning her attention to a drop of water that had somehow managed to travel across the room to land on the polished metal fridge door. The faint residue of chocolate trailed down the door. She shifted Jackie onto her hip and leaned against the breakfast bar separating the kitchen from the diner.

"No, I don't," said Liv, reaching to rescue the single rose bud Jackie had spied in the bud vase she had set on the breakfast bar. She was too late, and the bruised petals gave off their dying scent.

"I was hoping you wouldn't mind looking after him for a bit." Judy looked with distaste at the now bare rose stem poking out of the vase.

"Strange arrangement," she murmured, ignoring the rose petal still clinging to Jackie's pudgy fist.

"Really? Judy, who is he?" Liv rarely called her stepmother by her name, not even in private, although she had other names for her then, but usually referred to her simply as 'She'.

Judy finally focussed on Liv.

"He's your nephew."

Liv dropped the towel she had used to dry her hands, raised her eyebrows and stared at her stepmother.

"I'm pretty sure I don't have a nephew, Mamma. I have no siblings."

Judy carried Jackie into the living room and plonked him unceremoniously in the middle of the sofa, propped up by Liv's pristine cushions. He grunted and reached for a cake on the trolley and Judy absentmindedly handed him a chocolate covered petit fours. He promptly crammed it in his mouth, crumbs and cream spilling everywhere.

Judy dropped onto the sofa beside him, using another napkin in a vain attempt to contain the damage.

"A year before your father died, he told me about your birth. And about your sister. You have a twin."

"How? I lived with my mother until she died when I was five. I'd know if I had a sister, let alone a twin. And when Mum died, I came to live with you and Dad. He never told me I had a twin! How come I've suddenly got one now?"

Liv wiped the chocolate hand print off the coffee table, polishing the glass to its customary gleam. She tried to ignore the chocolate hand prints drying on her carpet, but failed. She gathered Laundress, white vinegar and warm water and carefully sponged the handprints, squatting elegantly, painfully aware that her linen skirt was creasing beyond repair. At least the chocolate was fading.

"For God's sake, Livvie, just sit!"

"I don't want it to stain," she said, pleased to see the chocolate had all but disappeared.

"So, no sister, no twin, no nephew."

Judy sighed and fiddled with the glove she still wore.

"Your father and I felt it best not to tell you. Your mother never told your father either, you know." She extricated each finger from the glove. She made a show of inspecting her manicured nails, ignoring Jackie's gurgles as he rolled over and let himself off the sofa.

"No you don't!" Liv swooped him up and, curiosity getting the better of her, she lifted him up to inspect his features close up.

He was very pale with big blue eyes framed with thick black lashes, barely-there eyebrows in a round face with chubby cheeks and a mop of light brown bouncy curls. He looked just like any other baby she had ever seen. Not that she had seen many. None of her friends had children and she was an only child of an only child – no siblings, no cousins, no nieces, no nephews. Her father had not even produced children with Judy and Liv was not even sure they had tried. Yet there was a familiarity about him. He reminded her a little of a photo she had seen of her father as a baby, but more recently as he had looked before he passed away from the cancer.

Now, with her father gone, the only family she had left was Judy, her stepmother.

"So where is this twin, then?" It sounded petulant and untrusting. It was.

Judy seemed even more interested in her nails,

picking at some nail polish that had managed to drip onto her skin.

"She's in a spot of bother – fallen on hard times."

"How did she know to contact you?

Jackie squirmed and rubbed his eyes, yawning and getting a little grizzly.

"He wants to sleep." Judy rummaged in the bag she had popped out of sight on the other side of the sofa and produced a bottle of milk.

"Mind if I warm this up?" Without waiting for a reply, she stood.

Liv followed her into the kitchen, still carrying the squirming, grizzling toddler. He had nestled his face in her neck. At first it was cute, but Liv felt the drool and shuddered. She would have to have a good long soak once this visit was over.

The microwave pinged and Judy removed the now warm bottle.

"Here," she said, thrusting the bottle in Liv's hand.

"What?" Liv recoiled as milk droplets escaped the teat and splashed both her and Jackie. She sighed, resigned to an impossibly creased skirt and now a milk-dappled shirt. She sank into the armchair opposite Judy, who sat on the sofa, and arranged Jackie so he was more comfortable. He took the bottle noisily, mewling at every gulp. Before the bottle was finished, he was asleep.

They sat in silence for a short while, neither being

sure what to say. Liv's mind was overflowing with questions; Judy's with the desire to get the information out.

"Shall I pour the tea?" It seemed easier to delay the inevitable a little longer and Judy rose to comply.

"The water will be cold."

"I'll boil the kettle, then," and with that, Judy disappeared into the kitchen.

Liv rested her head on the back of the chair, afraid to move to a more comfortable position in case she disturbed Jackie. She wracked her brain trying to make sense of this. Did she really have a sister, a twin? If so, why hadn't she heard about her before? Where was she? Who was she? She didn't even have a name, and without a name, she couldn't exist.

Judy returned with the kettle, adding it to the trolley, unbalancing the aesthetics. She poured the tea, spooning a generous serving of honey into her peppermint fusion, offering a raspberry and cranberry infusion to Liv.

"I don't usually play hostess to you!"

Judy blew delicately on the top of her tea and after taking a tentative sip (it was way too hot) she placed her cup and saucer on the coaster closest. Liv noted the gesture and their eyes met.

"So, I have a sister, huh?"

"A twin."

Perhaps to stall for time, or maybe just to give her

time to gather her thoughts, Judy took a delicate cucumber sandwich. She bit into it, revelling in the exquisite flavour and texture that only paper-thin cucumber slices and ultra-skinny bread slices with real butter between can achieve.

"Good," she said, her mouth full of the delicacy, and swallowed. "You've always been a good cook."

"Thanks."

This was leading somewhere, Liv knew it. She gently rearranged Jackie and took a sip of her tea. She had lost her appetite and hoped Judy had a big one.

"You know, it was your mother's choice to look after you alone, although she named your father on your birth certificate. And he wasn't actually there at your birth."

"I know. He told me." Liv sighed, exhausted. "But there's also a place for siblings on a birth certificate. Mine's blank."

"I know. And so is your sister's. But she also has a birth certificate naming your father as hers. And she was registered on the same day, same office even."

Liv digested this information, wondering how this could have not been caught by the Registry Office before now. It was a mystery that would probably remain unsolved. Liv sighed again.

"So how did she get in touch? With you, I mean."

"Long story." Judy bit into another cucumber sandwich. "Are you having any of these?"

Liv shook her head. "No appetite," she said.

"You have to eat."

"I'd rather know about my sister."

Judi sighed. "Not long after your father fell ill, she made contact. Asking for money, actually."

"Are you sure she's who she says she is?

Judy twirled her teacup in the saucer.

"Believe me. I was sceptical at first." She was silent for a minute, evidently looking for the words. "I know you've always thought of me as a gold digger."

When Liv went to protest, Judy held up her hand to forestall her. "It's okay. I may have thought the same about you, coming to us when your mother died, so I can understand why you might think that."

She was silent again and Liv looked closely at her, seeing her bottom lip quiver. At least, she thought she had seen it.

"No matter. We investigated her fully, believe me – hired a PI, had DNA tests ordered, you name it, we probably did it. She was legit. Your father bailed her out a couple of times after that. You know, Liv, you've really had it good compared to her. You had a relationship with your mother and then with your father. She had nothing."

"So where was she? Mum never mentioned I had a sister, and she would have known!"

'That was our real sticking point. Why would your

mother keep you and give up her? It didn't make sense. I didn't know your mum."

"No, but I did. And you're right. If there'd been another baby, she would have told me. That's what I'm so shocked about."

Jackie stirred in her arms and Liv gently rocked him until he settled again.

"From what we've been able to piece together, your mother had a rough time with your birth. She had a Caesar ..."

"I know about that. I saw the scars one day at the swimming baths and asked her. She told me it's where the doctor had to cut me out."

"In those days she would have been given a general anaesthetic, so may not have known about both babies. I'm thinking your mother's doctor, or perhaps the midwife, sold your sister to a family who wanted a baby.

"But the birth was registered – my parents named as hers. Doesn't make any sense."

"No, you're right, Livvie. It was your mother who registered both births. I've seen the original entries. Different signatures. Similar, but still different."

Liv frowned. "No one signs their name the same twice. Not even me, and God knows I've tried!"

"Do you remember how your mum used to sign her name?"

"Not likely! I was a kid!"

"Well, your birth registry entry is signed using 'Olivia Mansfield', quite distinct and easily read; your twin's as 'O Mansfield', or to be more precise OMans – followed by an elaborate swirl and a dot somewhere about the middle of the swirl."

"Do you have it here?"

Judy rummaged in her bag and took out a plastic wallet containing the birth certificate and a photocopy of the actual registry entries.

"I don't have yours, but the signatures are in the registry entries anyway."

Judy handed the papers to Liv, who still held the sleeping Jackie. She looked at the signatures closely, eyes squinting.

"The 'O' and 'M' are the same. Difficult to say for sure if mum signed them both, considering there's not really anything else to compare it to."

"Indeed. Your father was convinced. Shocked, of course."

There was silence between them for a few moments, broken only by the ticking of the clock and Jackie's steady soft breaths.

"Does she look like me? I mean, are we identical twins, do you think?"

"Spitting image. Your dad thought you were having a joke with him at first, except for the obvious fact that she was pregnant and you were not. There were other differences as well."

"Strange, but I always thought twins had a sort of bond. I've never felt like a part of me was missing, or that I have a bond with, well, anyone, really. Not my mum, not my dad or you. No one, really."

Liv shifted slightly to get comfortable. Who knew a sleeping toddler could weigh so much? He stirred a little in his sleep and Liv shushed him, rocking him gently, soothing him back to sleep. She was a mess. Her skirt was crumpled beyond recognition and along with the milk drops and drool on her shirt, there was now drool on her skirt, too. She wanted to lie him down on her sofa, but couldn't bear the thought of drool ending up there. At least her clothes were washable. Judy interrupted her introspection.

"I know I've been hard on you these past few years. I wasn't as convinced as your father that you weren't playing a game. I was sure if I came over at odd times, I'd catch you out."

"What? How?"

Judy flung her arm expansively, taking in the pristine surroundings. "You're a neat freak," she said. There was no emotion in her voice, just a matter-of-fact statement. "Your twin is not."

"Ah! So you were trying to catch me out? Did you think my standards had slipped?" Liv laughed, a mirthless sound with a deep-set bitterness. "I was taught by the best, you know. My mother was neat and tidy, but you!" She laughed again. "Mum had nothing on you. I never felt I could measure up. So I'm not sure if I get the 'neat-freak' habits from you or her!"

"Me, I guess."

"Nurture, not nature!"

Silence again, awkward this time.

"So, where's my twin now? Does she have a name?" She had been itching to ask, but in a strange way, did not really want to know. It was too much to take in at once.

Judy poured herself another cup of tea, spooned in some sugar and stirred for an endless time, staring at the teacup.

"She's ill, in a hospice. Jackie was dumped on me a week ago."

"Jackie's father?

She shrugged. "She didn't say."

Judy sipped her tea, which must have been quite cool. Jackie stirred again, stretched and opened his baby blues, staring straight into Liv's eyes. He gurgled happily and wriggled to a sitting position. Liv smiled in spite of her discomfort in holding the toddler. He really was quite sweet.

She stood and handed him back to Judy.

"He probably needs changing."

Without a word, Judy rummaged in her bag and extricated a blanket, which she spread on the sofa, and the necessary nappy-changing paraphernalia. She made quick work of changing him and handed him back to Liv.

"You should have done it – you can use the practice!"

"Whatever for? It's not like I'm going to have any kids anytime soon."

"Shall we go visit your sister?" Judy neatly sidestepped the comment.

"You've only just told me I have a sister. Not sure I'm ready to meet her!"

"She doesn't have much time."

Judy's comment cut the air and Liv, who had remained standing after taking Jackie back, found herself falling onto the sofa, surprising Jackie who looked up at her, his blue eyes questioning. She found herself holding the toddler close to her, a protective instinct she did not realise she possessed.

"She's terminal? And you're just telling me now?" It was a lot to take in. Liv rocked back and forth, comforting a toddler who at this point, really did not need it. It was soothing to her, though.

"I'll just change." Liv handed Jackie back and went to her room. Simple jeans and a sweater seemed appropriate. She stared at her reflection in the mirror in her bedroom for some time though.

What do you say to a sister who, up until an hour ago, you had no idea even existed? Liv thought, running her hands through her hair, gently tugging to ease the headache she could feel building. She stared at the haunted face looking back at her, wiping away minute smudges of mascara, smoothing the tension across her sinuses. She took a deep breath and re-joined her stepmother and Jackie.

"Let's go."

Liv had hated hospitals since her mother's death twenty years ago. It was not the smell of the bleach and disinfectant – they were comforting; it was the overall feeling of sickness and sadness that hospitals created in her. She followed Judy, who was now pushing Jackie in his stroller, as she walked straight to her sister's room, ignoring the looks of the nurses they passed sitting at the nurses' station at the entrance to the palliative care ward.

Nothing could have prepared her for this.

She stopped at the door of the room, staring in shock at the young woman who lay sleeping in the bed by the window. She was breathing through a tube. She was fed through a tube and a tube pumped fluids directly to her veins, and yet, underneath all that, she might just as well have been looking at a photograph of herself. She glanced up at the wall behind the bed and read that this was Kirsty. She finally had a name.

"Kirsty?" she called her name softly and tiptoeing to the bed, gently touched the pale, thin, bruised hand. There was no verbal response but a barely-there squeeze of her fingers. Liv swallowed, fighting an overwhelming emotion she had never thought possible to experience.

"Why leave it until now to tell me I have a sister?" she whispered, forcing Judy to meet her gaze.

"I told you. I wasn't convinced ..." Judy shook her head. "I am sorry, Liv."

"Does she know about me?" It had suddenly dawned on her that the shock might be too much for this dying young woman before her.

"I do, Liv." Kirsty's blue eyes, dim with pain, met Liv's. "Don't be hard on her. I didn't want you to feel obliged." She closed her eyes, taking slow, painful breaths.

"Sh. You don't have to explain."

"I know." She rested a little more. "How's my little man?"

Judy brought Jackie over to see his mum. He gurgled happily, reaching out to her.

"He's fine. See?"

"He doesn't know, poor little mite." She reached out to pat his hand. Jackie tried to climb onto his mother, but Judy had to hold him back.

"Not now, sweetie," she said, planting a kiss on his forehead.

"It's okay," Kirsty said, reaching for Jackie. "Just for a minute."

Judy gently lowered him so she could reach and

Jackie's pudgy little hand caressed his mother's face.

"Love you so much, Jackie-boy," Kirsty whispered.

She closed her eyes and for the longest moment there was no sound other than the steady beep of the monitors.

Liv struggled with her own emotions, really not knowing what to say. There was so much she wanted to know. What happened to Kirsty? Who looked after her? What was her life like? But these were questions for another day, although it did not look like there was going to be another time to ask. She lowered herself on to the chair beside the bed and gently took Jackie from Judy, sitting him on her lap so he could be near his mother without hurting her. He gurgled happily to himself, tapping his mother's face, her hands, if he strayed near to the tubes keeping her alive, Liv would gently guide them elsewhere.

Kirsty stirred again.

"Did I doze off again? I do that a lot." A tired grin waved across her face and she closed her eyes again for a second. "Liv," she said, "It's a lot to ask. I'm sorry."

"I ..." Liv looked at Judy, worry creasing her forehead. Judy shook her head and shrugged.

"Take Jackie?"

"Of course." Liv held Jackie closer to her, thinking how easily Jackie had taken to her today. She guessed the fact she looked like his mother may have had something to do with it, and yet he obviously knew the difference. For an uncoordinated toddler, he was incredibly gentle with his mother.

"I mean, when I'm gone. Can you look after Jackie? It's in my will. I wanted to be sure, though."

Liv swallowed hard, choking back the tears. "Kirsty, I don't know what to say? How can you ..."

"I'm sorry, I shouldn't have ..."

"... trust me? We've not met. I could be the worst person ..."

Kirsty laughed softly, wheezing with the effort. "I've known about you for a while – all of you. Just didn't have the courage to make contact earlier. Once I knew I had the dreaded C, I no longer had a choice." She dragged some more oxygen into her lungs and closed her eyes.

"Oh, Kirsty! I wish I'd known ..." Liv's throat tightened and the tears threatened to overflow. She inhaled a deep, shuddering breath. "If you're sure ..."

"I wouldn't be happy with him going anywhere else. You're blood."

Liv smiled at her through the tears that now rolled down her cheeks.

"I'll look after him as if he were my own."

It was late when she finally walked back in the door, carrying the now sleeping Jackie. He had cried a little when his mummy no longer spoke to him, sensing she was no longer there, but burying his little face into Liv's neck, his sobs had eventually subsided.

She had held him tightly to her, softly crooning through her own grief at the loss of a sister she never knew, and when the preliminary paperwork was done, Judy took her home via her own home to collect some of Jackie's things.

Liv gently laid him on the sofa, tucking cushions around him to keep him safe and covered him with his favourite blanket Judy handed her.

"I'll leave you to it," Judy said, handing her a bag with his most immediate needs. "I'll bring the rest over in the morning."

She leaned over to give her stepdaughter a hug.

"You'll be fine, you know."

"I know." She saw Judy out, locked the door and returned to the sofa.

It was a lot to take in. In one day she had found she had a sister, lost her sister and gained a nephew. She looked down at the sleeping child, fear and awe in her heart.

"I hope I can do you proud, Kirsty," she whispered. She turned down the lamp and drew a blanket over her shoulders. It was going to be a long night, but tomorrow would be a new day, a bright day of hope.

Bonnie and Claude

"Morning, Claude! Isn't it a glorious day outside?"

Bonnie slid over to the window and whipped open the black-out curtains, letting the glorious May sunshine enter the bedroom.

"Do you mind if I open the window? It's a lovely breeze out."

There was no response from Claude who still lay on his bed, staring up at the ceiling.

"You'll feel better if I do," she said, and threw open the sash window. A gentle breeze immediately played with the nets and the room was filled with the warm scent of roses from the garden and fresh mown hay drying in the meadow.

"I'll be in with some tea and toast for you in a bit."

Bonnie was used to his silences and left the room, gently closing the door behind her, so as not to destroy his reverie. She rummaged around in the kitchen, popping the kettle on, dropping a couple of pieces of bread in the toaster. She set up a tray, paying special attention to create an aesthetic display of her mother's old dainty tea-set, finishing it off with a bud vase and a single red rose.

She hummed softly to herself as she worked. It was good to be able to finally be able to do things that pleased Claude.

****

"Bonnie! Where's my supper?!"

Bonnie started at the shout, her heart pounding, adrenalin coursing through her body, causing her stomach to clench. Painfully.

"It'll be done in a minute," she called, fumbling in the drawer to find something to dish out the cottage pie and peas she had prepared. She had set the table, too, but she'd be sitting there alone. Either that or balancing her supper on her lap in front of the television like Claude did.

She thought perhaps she shouldn't complain about him so much. Not that she would actually say anything to anybody, of course. On the only occasion she had mentioned her marriage to anyone else, her mother had said: "You lie in your bed the way you made it." And that was the end of it.

Still, she saw the way the ladies at the church

beamed when their husbands came to sit with them in the hall after the service, dimpling, blushing brides, eager to latch on to every word that came out of their husbands' mouths. She, on the other hand, had followed Claude out of the hall, two steps behind, clutching her purse, rushing in her heels to keep up and then stumbling over the cobbles to the cottage they had once lived in on the edge of the village. They'd moved when it had become obvious she would never be able to provide Claude with a heritage. His family ended with her.

"Bonnie?!"

She sighed and picked up the tray delicately arranged with his tea and half a pint of ale. She set it down in front of him and left him to it, eating her solitary meal at the well-set table in the dining room.

****

"Here you go, love." Bonnie placed his breakfast on the side table before helping him to sit and plumping the pillows behind him. He was unsteady now and needed pillow support beside him as well. She had bought two long bolster cushions for the purpose and arranged them on either side to keep him from toppling over.

She lifted the tray and balanced it on his fragile knees, pouring him a cup of cooling tea, dropping in a cube of sugar and the tiniest splash of milk. He never used to like milk, or tea for that matter, but now he seemed grateful for whatever she did for him. He never complained, in any case.

She held the cup to his lips, but as usual, the liquid moistened his lips, nothing more. Bonnie sighed and spooned a bit of the tea directly into his mouth. His head didn't move, but his eyes turned to hers, unfathomable. Slowly he swallowed. Encouraged, she spooned in some more.

She broke off a morsel of the toast and placed it in his mouth. There was no reaction for a short while, but then Claude's mouth seemed to move of its own accord, he swallowed and the morsel was gone. She placed a straw in the tea cup and the toast back on the plate.

"I'll leave you to it, now, my love," she said. "Just nipping out to the store."

Bonnie collected her bag and left by the front door, carefully locking it behind her.

She hummed to herself again, a little tune she remembered from days long gone. It was still early, and the store would only just open as she arrived. There was no need to rush, so she strolled along the lane, passing the cottages as she went, greeting those who were already out, and wondering how anyone could be indoors on such a glorious day as she passed those cottages that were still asleep with their curtains drawn against the day.

"Morning Bill," she called out to the old man who lived a couple of doors down. His porch caught the morning sun and he always spent his mornings out there, sipping on his tea. It was Wednesday, today, so he had the added bonus of being able to read the small newsletter that passed for the village newspaper. He looked up from the gossip column.

"Morning, Bonnie. How's Claude?" Bill never used to ask after Claude in the old days, but ever since Claude had taken to his bed, it was surprising how many people had taken an interest in his well-being.

"He's up and about today," she said, just as she did every day, even though it had been months since Claude had actually left his bed of his own accord. And she would get him up once she came back from the store. He did seem to enjoy sitting out in their private back garden. At least, he never complained.

"I might pop over and see him later," said Bill.

Bonnie smiled. Bill always said that, but never did come.

Bill's wife, June, popped her head out of the front door and saw Bonnie.

"He likes to think he's still 19, you know," she said, shaking her head. "He'll not get out to see Claude any more than your Claude will come out to see Bill!" The two ladies exchanged knowing glances, acknowledging who really was the strong one in each of their relationships.

Bonnie knew Bill found it difficult to navigate the cobbled lanes. Just like Claude, he hadn't left his house for months. She nodded and continued on her way.

In the store, she purchased half a dozen eggs and a

lamb chop for her supper. No point wasting lamb on Claude. She'd do him a poached egg. She picked up some milk and a packet of biscuits for later. She didn't really need much, but she did like to go for a daily walk, and the store gave her the perfect excuse. Claude's illness had certainly given her a lot of freedom.

****

"Where do you think you're going?" Claude had been in a foul mood that day.

After all the years she had given up hope of ever having a baby of her own to love and cherish. But recently, following one of the infrequent sessions of 'love-making' where she had followed her mother's advice to simply "lie back and do it for England", she had noticed not-so-subtle changes in her body. Tender breasts and a constant feeling of nausea had driven her to seek her mother's advice. She called her on the party line and described her symptoms.

"You're probably pregnant." Her mother's matter-of-fact tone confirmed her fear. It's not that she didn't want a baby. Of course she did. Didn't every woman? It was that she didn't want to have a baby now. She was in her forties – late forties – and Claude was too set in his ways to be a daddy to a little baby.

"I'm just going to see my Mam. I'll only be gone a few days," Bonnie said. Her mother lived in the next county – not too far for a visit, but too far just to go for one day. She could really do with her advice on pregnancy. She was barely showing; the tender breasts,

nausea and a slight thickening of her waist the only signs as yet.

"I need you here," he'd shouted.

Normally she wouldn't have argued, but, blame it on the hormones, she was feeling belligerent, and perhaps even a tad reckless. She'd just shook her head, told him she was going, and walked out of the door.

The next thing she knew she was in hospital with an empty womb.

****

Bill was still sitting on his porch when she passed by on her way home, her shopping securely in the string bag she carried for the purpose. She waved. He nodded. Their own ritual.

Letting herself back in her front door, she poked her head around the door to Claude's room. He was asleep now, the soft moans testimony of the pain he still felt, despite the medication. She tiptoed in, gathered up his breakfast tray, and noted that today he had actually attempted to nibble more of his toast. His tea was half empty; no doubt aided by the straw he had been able to manage a few sips more.

She carried the tray to the kitchen and tidied it all away. The sun was now on her back porch and so she took an old romance novel and a cup of tea for herself out there.

"Bon!" Claude's fragile, hoarse cry barely reached into the romance, interrupting the lovers mid-tryst.

Bonnie sighed.

"Coming, love." She should have woken him up when she came home. No doubt he needed changing.

"Shall we get you ready?" She always made out he was going on a grand outing, and sometimes that was exactly what it felt like, bathing him, dressing him, sitting him in the 'day chair' while she changed his bedding. When all was done, she would help him up, either to stand him in front of his Zimmer frame, or, as was the case today, to lower him into his wheelchair.

She imagined this was how being a mother must have felt like, after a fashion. There were obvious differences, of course. After all, he was much heavier than a baby would have been, although lately he had lost more weight and it was no longer such a chore.

She chattered to him as she worked, telling him about the story he had interrupted, about her wander to the village store, that Bill had said he'd come over and that Bill's wife had said he wouldn't. She couldn't stop, even when she felt the slight pressure on her arm and, looking at Claude, could see his silent pleading for her silence.

He made her nervous, even now, as weak as he was. And when she was nervous, she chatted.

****

She was inconsolable for a long time after losing the baby. It was funny that she should feel that way, seeing as, by that time, she no longer wanted it. However, losing this baby had re-iterated the emptiness of her life. She was Claude's wife, but what did that mean? He didn't love her; did she love him? Possibly. But Claude was a tyrant.

He was different once she'd lost the baby, though. If he barely spoke to her before now he merely communicated in grunts and gestures. For her part, the less he spoke to her the more she prattled on. When he grew tired of her chatter, he simply walked away. Then she could relax and she spent many an evening alone, knitting and crocheting baby clothes for the child she would never bear.

She had just finished a pair of baby bootees the evening she heard about Claude's accident.

A sharp rap on the door coincided with the last stitch of the bootee. She pulled the yarn through the loop, rendering it finished, wove it back through a few stitches and snipped it. There was another rap on her door. She sighed and forced herself to answer the door.

A tall policeman and a diminutive lady stood on her doorstep.

"Can I help you?"

It was the woman who responded.

"Mrs Beaumont," she said, crisp, no nonsense. "I'm afraid we have some bad news. Can we come in?"

Bonnie frowned, shook her head and shrugged her shoulders. "Of course." She led them into her parlour, motioning for them to sit.

The lady perched on the edge of the sofa. The policeman took Claude's chair.

"Would you like some tea?" Bonnie remembered her manners. "Claude says I should always offer tea, even though he doesn't like it himself. He's more a lager drinker, or whisky ... not tea though ..."

She fell silent, knowing she was prattling, knowing Claude would tell her off for that when he found out. When both the policeman and the lady declined the tea, she slipped onto the armchair.

"Mrs Beaumont" the lady began, "there's been an accident. At the mine."

"Is there anything I can do to help?"

The policeman and the lady exchanged glances. The man cleared his throat, opened his mouth to speak, then closed it again. He gestured to the lady.

"Mrs Beaumont," she began again, "your husband has been in an accident at the mine."

"I don't think so. Have you got the right Mrs Beaumont? Claude's brother's wife lives a few miles on the other side of the mine but I don't think John works in the mine. Claude's sister's boy, Charlie, does. She's not a Beaumont any more, though. My Claude doesn't work down the mine. He works in the city. He's in finance ..."

Her prattling trailed off at the upraised hand from the policeman and she flinched a little. Silly, really. She didn't think he was going to hurt her.

"Mrs Beaumont," it was the man speaking now, "where does your husband work?"

"Well," her eyes darted to the window, then to the door, then to the portrait of her and Claude on their wedding day. It was a happy day. "He's a clerk. In finance. In an office. Works for the Council, I should think."

The policeman raised an eyebrow at the woman on the sofa.

"Ma'am," he said, "your husband is in the hospital. There was an explosion. It was at the end of the shift and most of the workers had already left. Your husband was rounding up the stragglers and was the last to leave."

"He's not … ?"

"He's alive." The lady smiled, leaned forward and clasped Bonnie's cold hands in her warm ones.

"Well, that's something." Bonnie sighed. "Is he okay?"

"He is at the moment. We're not sure of the, er, what the doctors say he'll be like, if he … you know, once he recovers."

Bonnie nodded. "I guess I'll need to see him."

"We're here to take you now."

"I'm sure I could take myself."

"I'm sure you could but we're here to support you." The lady's crisp tone was not particularly supportive.

For once, Bonnie had nothing to say.

The policeman stood and extended a hand to Bonnie. "Ma'am, if you'd like to grab your coat."

Bonnie ignored the policeman's hand and rose with elegant grace from the armchair. Her coat and handbag were on the hat stand in the hall.

Bonnie didn't really know how she felt when she saw Claude lying in that hospital bed, his bruised face almost unrecognisable, a machine breathing for him.

"Doesn't look like he'll be okay."

The nurse tending to his wounds paused in her ministrations.

"The doc will be able to give you a better idea."

On cue, the surgeon entered the room and took Bonnie aside.

"The way I see it, you have a choice. At the moment, we're keeping him alive. I can't be sure, but his prognosis isn't good. He'll certainly never be able to walk again and will need constant care."

"What are his options?" It was a whisper.

****

She had come to regret her decision to take him off life-support.

Claude was a proud man, strong-willed and defiant. If she thought he was going to slip peacefully away once the doctors had switched off the machine, she had another think coming. If he could order her to tend to his every whim, his continued longevity meant she had to tend to his every need. He could do very little for himself.

If Bonnie had known then that Claude would survive the pulling of the plug, she may have chosen differently. At least while he was comatose in the hospital, he was someone else's responsibility. He defied the odds and lived, although he never regained the use of his body.

What kind of life was this, though, totally dependent on, even at the mercy of, the one person he used to control.

As his full-time carer Bonnie thought her life had taken a turn for the worse and for a time it had. As the weeks and months turned into years, however, she realised a new freedom she had never before experienced, not even as a child. Claude still may not approve of anything she did, but what did it matter? He could not do anything about it.

And so, although she never left him for very long, she found she had so much time to devote to activities she had once only dreamed of. Her needs were simple, though; a good book to read, something to occupy her hands, and a clean house.

After settling Claude in clean clothes in his chair by the window, Bonnie returned to the life of love and luxury lived vicariously in the romance novel she had discarded earlier when Claude called her in.

The sun had set and it was a little cool outside by

the time Bonnie finished the book. She snapped it shut, dried her eyes and stretched a little.

"I guess I should get some supper organised," she said, slowly easing her old, aching body to a standing position.

She took out the lamb chop and vegetables she had purchased earlier and set them to cook, along with a poached egg for Claude.

"Here, love," she said, carrying in the meagre meal along with another cuppa.

She helped him back into his bed after changing his bags and fed him his egg and tea. He looked comfortable enough and after giving him a quick peck on his papery cheek, Bonnie left him staring at the ceiling.

Her tea was a little over-done by the time she made it back to the kitchen. She nibbled on the lamb chop, ate a little of the mash and totally ignored the now soggy vegetables. She cleaned up after tea and settled down on the sofa to watch a little telly before taking herself off to bed.

****

Claude awoke to a room filled with sunlight. He lay uncomfortably on his back, listening to the normal house noises, trying to determine where she was. He could hear the television playing out an old daytime drama and so assumed Bonnie was in the living room.

It was unusual for her to be doing so. Television was an evening thing. It was one of the rules. He turned his neck so that he could see the side table and saw that she hadn't left him anything to eat. The discomfort of the bag told him she had not been in to him at all. Although ordinarily he did not eat much, perhaps because Bonnie was late, he found he was rather hungry and extremely thirsty.

Life for Claude had certainly not turned out the way he had expected. Ever since the accident at the mine, he knew Bonnie now knew his secret. He was a failure! He was no hotshot accountant in the city. Just a miner, like his family before.

And yet, despite the lies and the violence, Bonnie had still chosen to look after him. He knew she had opted to have his life support stopped when it looked like he was going to die, and in fact, he had willed her to do so. He had not wanted to live like this. However, he had rallied and the doctors changed their tune and said he would recover. But he had not – not fully.

The fullness of his bladder and bowel was now very uncomfortable. "This is not like Bonnie at all." He thought.

"Bon?" he called out to her, but his voice was raspy and dry and the sound barely left his room. He swallowed, trying to muster some saliva to lubricate his mouth and vocal cords.

"Bon!"

There was no response.

It was such a little effort, but it tired him and he sank into his pillows, breathing heavily. After a few minutes, he decided to try to move, but the years of inactivity and weakness had not improved his stamina. He had managed to roll over, but that only served to trap his arm underneath his body. Tears of frustration escaped, and he did not have the strength to wipe them away.

****

Claude had no idea how long he had lain like that, but eventually the room darkened and evening fell. His bags had burst and he lay in a pool of his own excrement. The stench was overpowering but he was helpless, totally at Bonnie's mercy.

"Bon!" He called out again, but now his voice was muffled. He could barely breathe and finally slipped into slumber.

****

"Claude?"

He opened his eyes and was surprised to find himself sleeping in a clean bed in a clean white room. Lacy curtains danced in the cool early morning summer breeze, bringing with it the smell of fresh cut hay and wildflowers. He sat up in bed, surprised at how easy it was to move today. He was totally pain-free.

"That was one brilliant sleep! I feel so alive!"

He swung his legs off the bed and slipped his feet

into the soft slippers he found there. A beautiful young Bonnie stood in front of him.

"You must have had a good sleep, too, Bon." He patted the bed beside him. "Come, sit with me."

Bonnie hesitated, glancing out of the window at the familiar fields now bathed in glorious sunshine.

"I don't understand..."

She shook her head and, ignoring his invitation to sit beside him, walked to the open window and leaned outside.

"This is home, and yet ..."

She looked back and saw an echo of her former life, Claude, at once sitting on the edge of his bed, but also the fragile mound of humanity he had become and slowly it dawned on her. She gasped, covering her mouth with her hands to stifle the sound. She looked at him and then ran out of the room to her own room.

Her room was empty and undisturbed. Realisation dawned as she explored the rest of house. It was immaculate, just the way she had left it last night. She paused in front of the hall mirror and was not surprised by what she saw there.

Then, moving into the living room, she saw herself, the old lady she had become, sleeping peacefully on the sofa. Softly she approached the sleeping woman and was surprised to feel a warm wetness on her cheeks. She reached forward and stroked the old woman's cheek.

"You did so well," she whispered.

A movement out of the corner of her eye caught her attention and she saw the Claude she once knew, joining her in the room.

"I am so sorry for the hell you've lived with me, Bon," he said putting his arm around her shoulders.

Bonnie was about to answer, but was interrupted by a strange mewling sound.

"A baby?" she whispered. She followed the sound to the spare room and lifted the bundle which was cocooned in a cradle. Fresh tears coursed down her cheeks.

"We've been given a second chance," she whispered.

****

It had been uncommonly warm, but that usually would not have stopped Bonnie from taking her daily walks to the village store. Bill missed seeing her and had finally convinced June to come with him to check.

It was the flies around the house that first told June and Bill that all was not okay at Bonnie and Claude's, but the smell was a dead giveaway. The front door was closed but not locked, and after receiving no response to their knocking, they went in.

They found Claude in his bedroom, lying face-down in a pool of his own excrement. Bonnie they found resting on the sofa, staring with unseeing eyes at the midday movie – Bonnie and Clyde.

Chemical Imbalance

Cindy

I first met Nigel on a dating show. He was Bachelor Number One. I had no idea what he looked like, but his voice! My knees buckled as he answered my questions with his deep bass that sent shivers up my spine. My questions were a little suggestive, I have to admit, but it's all in good fun, isn't it?

When the screen was drawn back and he was revealed, I was disappointed. His face and voice didn't match. It's not that he was bad looking, because he wasn't, but, well, I guess I was expecting an Adonis but instead, well, you get the picture.

I know it's customary for the Bachelorette to give her Bachelor a kiss when they meet and I went to give him a peck on the cheek. Ugh! So gross! He turned his face at the last minute, grabbed my head and pulled me into him for a slobbery snog. The crowd loved it and, after my initial disgust, I played along. I was sick afterwards. Physically sick. Everything I had eaten or drank up to that point left me like a fountain.

Gross. Just gross.

Nigel

I was lucky when I first met Cindy that the other contestants on *Blind Date* were such bores. We, of course, all knew what she looked like, and although I'm not really attracted to women with big hair, big bones and big boobs, she was bubbly and entertaining, so I decided to give it my best shot. Besides, my recent dates had all left me dead so from that perspective, just about anyone would have done. I don't really have a type as such. Docile and submissive. I guess it doesn't really matter what that looks like.

Cindy was neither docile, nor submissive so I was really going out of my comfort zone here.

To be fair to my rivals, though, they had nothing to counteract my obvious charm. Remember, I could see them. I knew who the competition was, and let's face it, on these shows, we have to **sound** good, otherwise the dame behind the screen is never going to pick us.

I could tell from her questions that she wanted what I could give her. She was flirty, suggestive, laughed, perhaps a little hysterically, at my answers and we could hear she was getting a little hot under the collar. Her breathing had accelerated, and we all know that means arousal.

And when she did choose me and we saw each other for the first time, I could tell she was as smitten with me as I was with her. I pulled her into a passionate embrace and we stayed like that, snogging on national television, hell, international television for all I knew, for a full minute. The studio audience loved it. They cheered and catcalled, wolf-whistled and stamped their feet, calling out things like: "On yer, mate!" and "Give her one for me!"

We both enjoyed that kiss, I could tell. I could feel her heart pounding against my chest and I have to say, nothing turns me on more than to feel blood pumping …

I was in heaven.

Cindy

So, fast forward to our date. Well, it was against my better judgement that I agreed to go on this date with Nigel, anyway. I can't fault the location – a weekend in London, flying business class from New York and staying at the fancy Shangri-La Hotel. This was amazing and I'd always wanted to go to London. I guess I like a bit of the high class and the first thing we were supposed to do when we arrived – well, after settling into our hotel – was to catch a Shakespeare play at The Globe. What an opportunity!

We had arrived in plenty of time and our guide was supposed to collect us from the Hotel at four o'clock that afternoon and take us on a leisurely stroll through Borough Market, along Bankside and the Thames River, across Southwark Bridge into Zizzi's for pizza, before going to the performance of Romeo and Juliet at seven thirty. Well, that didn't happen.

The guide was ready and I was ready, but Nigel! I don't know what that man was doing because to be honest, he looked no different than he did when we got off the plane at Heathrow hours before, but, despite me, the guide, and the inevitable camera crew (remember, this date was courtesy of *Blind Date*) taking our turn at nudging him along – with no response from his closed door, I might add, he didn't come downstairs until seven o'clock, half an hour after the performance was due to start.

We didn't get to see the show.

Nigel

I thought dates were supposed to be fun, you know, what the guy and gal decide to do together, but this one. Seriously! It was all mapped out for us before we even left the JFK airport. I know it was a game show win, okay? But surely we could still get a say in what we do? Shakespeare! Who wants to see a play about two teenagers who kill themselves because they think they're in love?

When we got to the hotel I looked out of my

window, straight onto a view of cranes and the like from what was obviously a building under construction. I called downstairs immediately for them to change my room to one with a view, which they kindly obliged. I will say this for the English, they are incredibly good butlers.

After changing rooms, I was feeling hungry so ordered room service and ate what the English think is a burger. Not in my book! I guess it tasted just fine, but it was served on a plate with a knife and fork and in two halves. I just squished them both together and threw it down with a chug of warm lager. Not ice-cold. Disgusting.

I had a spot of ketchup or whatever passed for it, on my shirt and had to wash that out before the date, so did so, and then used the hair dryer to dry it. It looked okay. By the time I was done it was nearly 6:30. I thought it best to clean my teeth, so did that, made sure my hair looked the same as it did when I arrived – perfect – and I was finally ready to go.

They were all waiting for me in the Lobby and the guide gave me a funny look. I shrugged, took my date's arm, although to be honest, jeans and a sweater to a fancy theatre just doesn't seem right. I'm sure my trousers, buttoned up shirt, tie and sports coat (which I decided to wear just in case the ketchup was obvious) was a better choice. I guess it didn't really matter as we never made it to the theatre.

Cindy was a good sport about it, very polite. I do like a girl who knows her place.

Cindy

I guess the evening wasn't a total write-off. We did get to have a tour of the Globe after the performance and were still able to meet the actors and talk to them. It would have been better to talk about the actual performance, though. Also, the restaurant was kind enough to let us have our meal, even though we had clearly missed our booked slot. Very gracious, indeed.

We took a walk along the Thames after dinner. This will never be disappointing. I love lights reflecting on water and what a brilliant view from the Millennium Bridge, as is the view of St Paul's of course. Such famous landscapes and so close to me! He wanted to hold my hand as we walked and I didn't see the harm in it. His hands, though, were clammy and I had to just grin and bear it. The date might not be working for me, but at least I'm getting to see a part of the world I had dreamed about as a child.

I thought I'd get up early the next day and go and see Borough Market for myself, before the first scheduled event, but I forgot we were supposed to have breakfast together. I chose a full English – that was something we actually had in common, but other than that, I'm afraid for me the date was a wash-out.

I forgot to mention that he tried to recreate our first kiss when we finally arrived back at the hotel. He walked me to the door of my room. I told him he didn't need to bother seeing as we were in a safe hotel, but he insisted. This should have been sweet, but no.

I opened my door and turned towards him to say goodnight and he pushed me into my room, grabbed the back of my head and forced our faces close together, crushing my lips against his teeth. I think I cried out something, can't really remember, but I suddenly felt a shove from behind – the door, I think – pushing me even closer to him, but then I was held from behind and he was dragged away from me.

It was our guide holding me and the cameraman dragging him away, saying "She didn't invite you in, buddy," or something like that.

I tasted blood on my lip and sucked on it to hide it from everyone. He scared me a little. I can take care of myself, usually, but he took me by surprise. Perhaps he forgot we were still being filmed. It was the weirdest date, I have to say. I was grateful for the crew members' intervention.

Breakfast was awkward and I think at that point, I was ready to go home.

Nigel

I was so happy we hadn't had to sit through a stuffy play written by a dead man. The rest of the evening was lovely. We held hands as we strolled along the waterfront. I could see every man we passed thinking what a lucky sod I was, to be out with such a beauty. A guy likes to think he has something other men want, it makes him feel big and important. That's me, I guess; Big and Important.

She seemed to know every landmark we passed and gave a bit of a running commentary – "that's the Tate Modern behind us", "we're walking on the Millennium Bridge, made famous by Harry Potter" whoever that is, and "don't you just love the dome of St Paul's and how wonderfully it's framed – the bridge leads directly to it." I just nodded and made appropriate noises, happy just to hear her sweet voice. I could feel that we had made a connection and I was thinking it might be a good idea to take this date further, you know, go on more, get to know her more, maybe even go to the next level here. In London.

I didn't want anyone to know I'd switched rooms so I offered to walk her to her room. After all, that's what I would have done on a normal date, you know, one without the cameras rolling. The guide and cameraman were having a bit of a conversation, so I decided we should go up now and steered Cindy in the direction of the lifts. She came with me willingly enough, and when we got to her room, she told me "goodnight", but her eyes said "come inside" and so I pulled her to me and we kissed. She was moaning, obviously enjoying it and so we made our way inside. I have no idea what happened then. She seemed to push herself on me even harder and I nearly lost my balance. I then felt someone grab me and pull me away, saying "We'll have none of that here, buddy," or something like it.

He frogmarched me out of the room and pushed me towards the door across the hall. That was my old room, but he opened the door and pushed me inside. My stuff was there, so I was a tad confused. I called the desk but they insisted there was no mistake and so I had to stay in the room without a view.

In the morning, we met for breakfast and it was like nothing bad had happened at all. She was all smiles and we both ordered the full English breakfast. I would have preferred toast and coffee, but I wanted to let her know we were the same.

I was looking forward to seeing what we'd be doing today. We had the morning to ourselves and could do what we wanted. After breakfast, though, she left me in the restaurant and I have no idea what happened to her after that.

Cindy

I didn't think I could get through another day with Nigel so I looked out for the tour organiser and discussed this with her and the cameraman. We agreed they'd keep him out of my way for the rest of the day and I'd be able to see a bit of London on my own. I opted to go with my original plan and visited Borough Markets. I'd heard about it and wanted to sample some of the European delicacies, and maybe even bring home a trinket or two. There would, of course, be the obligatory fridge magnet!

I was enjoying my solitude when I heard my name

being called. Odds are it wasn't Nigel, although it did sound like him and a New York twang in the midst of these English accents was rather distinctive. I hope it didn't look like I heard him. I kept walking at the usual pace and hoped I'd be able to lose him in the crowd.

No such luck. At least we'd be going home tonight and I would never have to see him again.

Nigel

I waited for her to return to the table, thinking she had just gone to 'powder her nose', but when she hadn't come back after half an hour, I thought maybe she'd got lost. I went to find the organisers but they hadn't seen her either.

I thought I may as well go to Borough Markets. She'd said she wanted to go there on the way to Shakespeare last night, so maybe she'd decided to go after all. She could have told me. I'd have loved to have gone with her.

I eventually saw her at a bread stall, sampling some of the local wares. I called out to her, but it's a busy place and I guess there was too much noise for her to hear me. She moved off and I ran after her, pushing through the crowd as best I could without being too brash.

I finally met up with her and we continued to leisurely browse the stalls, hand in hand. It was a match made in heaven.

She bought a few silly fridge magnets – to commemorate her trip, apparently, and all too soon, we needed to head back to the hotel to pack for the return journey. I planned to make the ride home memorable for both of us. There was a certain club I was eager to join!

Cindy

The good thing I could take away from my walk through Borough Market with Nigel is that it marked the end of our date. I now just needed to endure the flight home. Luckily we hadn't exchanged phone numbers or addresses so once I walked away from him I would never have to see him again. Oh, except for the show after the date, but I might be lucky and be able to get out of it. I really don't think I could stand to be in front of the cameras with him again.

I saw our tour guide as we walked back into the hotel and the apologetic look on her face was unbearable. I hope I managed to convey in my expression that I didn't blame her. I had, after all, mentioned my desire to see the Market although he had equally expressed his disdain for such an idea. She came up with me to help me pack and the cameraman went with Nigel.

Once we were safely in my room, she grovelled for my forgiveness. I told her I knew it wasn't her fault but begged her to find me a seat on the plane as far away from Nigel as possible. She grinned and told me it was already done. I'd be flying first class! I hugged her and we lugged my bags down in the lift. I was in the best mood I'd been all weekend.

Nigel

Well, that was a date to remember. I grinned at the tour guide when we arrived back at the hotel and gave her a very sneaky thumbs up. I'd found Cindy!

The cameraman and I made our way up to my room to collect my belongings. Not sure why he had to come as well. It's not like I had a lot of stuff to bring down. Maybe the hotel insisted to make sure we didn't steal their towels, or the soap! As if.

I told the cameraman that this was the best date I'd been on. He wasn't very talkative, but I'm sure he appreciated my thanks for his part in the weekend. I told him I was looking forward to flying home and for the time Cindy and I would have to get to know each other better. I gave him a wink but he just rolled his eyes. I'm sure he knew what I meant.

I carried my bag downstairs. The cameraman took the lift. This was a terrific weekend and the first of many more to come, I'm sure.

Cindy

Well, that was an experience I'd not care to repeat. True to her word, the tour guide had managed to secure me a first class ticket. What neither of us realised was that there was no difference in this flight between first and business classes and as luck would have it, I was stuck with Nigel again.

I didn't feel comfortable doing this, but, after he'd made some suggestion about how we could join the Mile-High club, I feigned fatigue and spent the rest of the nearly seven-hour journey pretending to be asleep – after a quick trip to the bathroom alone and a word in the ear of the tour guide to make sure he didn't touch me while I slept. I hope she kept her word, but I did doze off for quite some time and woke feeling violated. I'm just not sure if that's because he was so close. I shudder when I think of it now.

Nigel

Well, that didn't go according to plan. Seems the weekend had tired her out and she wasn't up for a bit of mile-high adventure. Still … well, I got what I could manage, if you get my drift. What she doesn't know won't hurt her, eh?

Cindy

It's been a few months after that disastrous date. I'm sure the little weasel copped a feel while I was asleep but I can't prove it. I've not heard from him, although I suspect he may have managed to get my phone number at least. I've had a few prank calls where there was no one there when I answered.

Although the date itself was such a disaster, I have to tell you, what I later found out is even more disastrous, or had the potential to be so.

I was watching the news last night and a section came on about a man who was accused of murdering his date and lo and behold, who should be dragged out of the back of the police car but Nigel. I mean, I'm sure it's him. His hair was longer and more unkempt than when I had last seen him, but those chiselled features – it was definitely him.

I choked on my soda as my phone rang. There was no one there again. Surely he wouldn't waste a phone call on me?

Last Moments in Time

"What? Up already?" Ruth called to the couple seated at the patio setting just outside the kitchen window of the quaint little cottage by the sea.

"I'll put the kettle on then."

The crows were particularly vocal this morning, congregating on the giant poinciana in the back garden. Frank had planted that tree on their wedding day so many years ago and its gnarled trunk twisted and turned heavenward, reflecting their many struggles and overall triumphs. Her children had played in that tree, and their children too, for a while. Nobody played there now. Nobody but the crows.

Her hands were as gnarled as the tree trunk. Used to such menial labour, they busied themselves at the pump, filling the kettle and replacing the whistler on its end.

"I hope the noise won't bother you," she said. "I'm finding it a bit hard hearing things these days and the whistle is just enough to get my attention."

She placed the kettle on the stove, and then opened the door to set the fire. Dry kindling, twigs and an assortment of thicker pieces were already laid neatly in the fire box, ready for the match.

"Thanks for setting the fire for me, love," she called to the titian-haired woman. "You're a real dear."

She struck the match and the flame caught the dry kindling with a satisfying crackle. Soon the fire was well under way. She closed the fire door and bustled about in the kitchen, preparing the breakfast things.

Cracked cups and saucers lined the hutch, but hidden behind the rubble was her prize. The exquisite rose Dalton tea set once belonged to someone very special, though the years had eroded the memory until only the impression of a beautiful slender girl remained. She had long since given up trying to remember her name, but the memory of such poignant beauty and goodness always brought a sigh to her withered lips. A tear escaped her tired eyes and rolled down her leathery cheek, falling like a dew drop on the dust accumulating on the bench.

With papery palms, she brushed the tear away and set the tea cups on the battered serving tray. Carefully she measured the tea leaves into the pot - enough for three very weak cups, and added the cream jug and the sugar bowl. Delicate silver teaspoons and, because today was special, some of yesterday's shortbread completed the repast.

"Ah, a watched pot never boils," she reminded herself, after feeling the kettle and finding it barely warm. She popped her head out the back door.

"I'll just slip inside and do a quick tidy up of the bedrooms and the parlour," she called out, and scuttled out of the kitchen to do just that.

The front bedroom was light and airy with the early morning sun glinting through the curtains. A light sea breeze danced with the flimsy gauze to the accompaniment of a crystal chime. Ruth's bed was a little girl's dream - white four-poster with a lacy coverlet and fluffy pillows reflecting feminine delicacy. Around the room an assortment of teddy bears, dolls and soft toys completed the picture of child-like innocence. On the dresser beside her bed, a glass of water and the various pills she now needed to keep her heart beating, seemed strangely out of place and a photo of a much younger woman glared out of its frame, daring the observer to find anything wrong with the scene.

She smoothed the covers and rearranged the pillows. There was really not much to do, and she had already made the bed However, the chance to once again enter her room filled her with a delight she was sure she had not felt in a long time. Certainly, as a little girl, the room she had shared with her four sisters was nothing like the one she now occupied.

Another sigh escaped.

"Onward and forward," she quipped as she shuffled to the second bedroom.

The door was shut and she struggled with the old catch. It finally released, and the rusty hinges squealed in protest.

A dank odour greeted her and momentarily caught her off balance.

"How can she possibly sleep in here with that smell?" she asked herself. "Never mind. I'll soon have it back to normal."

She threw aside the curtains and tried to force the window open. It was stuck, but her movement had created eddies and whirlpools as the disturbed dust settled. Humming to herself, she began to straighten the room, stopping short when she noticed the tidiness of the bed.

"You shouldn't have gone to the trouble," she called out. There was no answer, though she didn't expect one. For such a small cottage, sound didn't travel all that well. She was about to dust the dressing table when a photograph lying loose on the bedside table caught her eye.

"Why, I haven't seen this photo in years," she whispered to herself. "Emily must have brought it with her."

The faded photograph, taken so many years ago, of a family group in the garden, stirred vague memories. Ah, yes, there she stood in her favourite blue dress with the red beads. The silly hats she used to wear. "My, how fashions change," she giggled to herself, remembering how she had taught her children the Charleston while they were still young enough to think her beautiful and all-knowing.

Next to her was Frank holding Emily. She was such a beautiful little girl. Her curly hair flowed around her head like a halo, especially when the sun turned the auburn into burnished copper. And when she smiled, two deep dimples popped into her cheeks and brought a smile to whoever saw them. Her older children were arranged in various heights around their parents and all were dressed in their Sunday best. Things change, and babies grow up and move away, some never to return as their busy lives take over.

"In those days we dressed up for a portrait," she murmured to herself.

The sudden whistling of the kettle brought her back to the present.

"Don't worry, Em. I'll get it," she called, and shuffled back to the kitchen.

Balancing the tea tray in one hand, Ruth pushed the door open with the other.

"Here we are then," she said, laying the tea cups neatly on the patio table. "It's a beautiful morning, isn't it? And so warm for this time of year."

She poured the tea into the three cups, and out of habit, added their cream and sugar. The shortbreads she placed at the centre of the table.

"Help yourselves," she said, and unsteadily brought her own cup to her lips.

The ringing phone startled her and she nearly dropped her tea.

"Heavens!" she exclaimed. "I'll never get used to that thing!"

Slowly she eased her tired old body out of the seat and answered the phone in the parlour. Seeing the dust on the mantelpiece reminded her of the task she had set herself that morning, so she painstakingly moved every ornament off the whatnot, the pelmets, the sideboard and the piano. Each piece held a special memory for her so the chore took a little longer than expected.

The mantle clock chimed the hour. It was already lunch time and she hadn't even finished breakfast. And then she remembered her guests.

"Oh, Emily!" she cried as she hobbled as fast as her tired old legs would carry her. "I forgot you came to visit us!"

Ruth opened the screen door and nearly tripped over the stoop in her haste to satisfy the needs of her guest.

"I'm so sorry. I've neglected you."

Busily, she gathered up the tea things.

"I'll make us a spot of lunch, and then we'll have the whole afternoon to chat. Won't that be lovely?"

And Ruth brought the cold tea cups, saucers and

untouched shortbread inside.

As she busied herself preparing a meagre lunch, it never occurred to her to ask for help. She always prepared the meals and looked after the children. It was her job, and Frank brought in the money. Not that he was doing very well at that lately. Still, she could manage. Isn't that what her mother told Frank on their wedding day?

"You'll find Ruthie very good at making do with what she has," she said. "You'll live like kings and queens no matter what you bring in." And her father had added his own tuppence...

"See that you don't spoil her, my boy. She's used to doing without."

But Frank was a good provider and they had lived like royalty. He bought them the little cottage by the sea in the early years of marriage while Ruth was still pregnant with their first son. All their children were born in this house.

It was all in the past now, though it seemed like yesterday.

"Be out in a minute, love," she called, as though in answer to a query.

Only the raucous caw of the crows in the poinciana tree answered her. Unperturbed, Ruth made a couple of sandwiches, reheated the tea in the pot and, with the tray once again full, carried her load out to the patio.

"There you go, love," she said, poured the tea and sat down.

She was still sitting there when the sun went down behind the mountains and the first stars appeared in the clear velvet sky. A chilled breeze blew in off the water, wafting through the open front door, down the central hallway and out to the patio.

Ruth shivered and shook herself free of her thoughts. The crows had long since gone, and so had the sandwiches she had made, but never touched. Her two guests remained as motionless as they had all day, neither eating, nor drinking. They weren't much company any more.

Resolutely, she picked them up, first Emily, and then Frank. They were heavier than she remembered when she first brought them out here.

"You'll be more comfortable in here," she told them, taking them into the second bedroom. She laid Emily on the bed and arranged her comfortably, pulling up the blankets and tucking them in tightly around her. Frank she stood by the window.

"Now, you keep on eye on Emily while she sleeps," Ruth admonished. His silence signified acquiescence.

Not bothering to lock the house, Ruth went into her own room. The window was still open and the night air chilled her old bones. Still, she refused to close it, preferring to breathe deeply of the fresh tangy sea air. Changing into a flimsy nightgown, she slipped beneath the covers, comforted by the soft pillows and cushions around her. She closed her eyes and slept.

In the front bedroom, the small frail figure was oblivious to the call of the crows on her poinciana tree as they greeted the dawn. Inside, the clock on the mantelpiece chimed the hour. Then all was silent.

In the second bedroom, Frank stood, an eternal guard over his precious Emily while the empty shell that was Ruth, slept on.

Mixed Messages

I met Paula at one of those toffy-nosed functions I rarely attend but often feel obligated to do so. I was bored out of my brain as I invariably am, nursing a soda water and trying to look interested in the woman monopolising my attention.

Out of the corner of my eye, a vision in a figure-hugging, long, black dress adorned with a diamond pendant on a thick, gold chain caught my attention. The flaming red hair, slender, stocking-clad limbs peeking through the mid-thigh split in her dress and graceful neck completed this vision of loveliness. I was stunned and am ashamed to admit my usual politeness and consideration for potential clients deserted me. I don't remember excusing myself from my boring companion but I was suddenly by the side of the most glamorous, seductive woman I had ever seen. We shared introductions and engaged in a conversation that continued 'til the end of the function, and then, totally out of character, I offered to escort her home.

Her eyes twinkled and I was sure she was going to accept when she fished a set of keys out of her handbag.

"Thanks, Hon," she drawled in that honey-sweet voice of hers, "but I have my car. Why don't I drive you home?" She settled those tawny lioness eyes on me and I couldn't refuse. So Paula drove me home to my Crown Street Townhouse in a sleek black Porsche, refused my invitation for a nightcap, and spun the wheels - elegantly - as she left. We did, however, exchange phone numbers, but something in her manner prevented me from calling her. I was sure I would never set eyes on her again.

I awoke Monday morning to the persistent sound of the phone ringing, rolled onto my side and stared in disbelief at the clock. I had forgotten to set the alarm. Groggily, I reached for the phone and mumbled a greeting.

"Good morning, Sleepyhead." The mellow, honeyed tones were like a splash of cold water on my face. "Sorry to disturb your sleep."

(At this point I really didn't care. I was speechless with shock and pleasure, and anticipation. She called me! Surely this was a good sign!)

"Are you free this Friday night?" Free? Friday? Of

course. I told her as much, trying to keep the excitement out of my voice, and we arranged to meet at the pub on the corner at eight. I offered to collect her but she reminded me she had a car, and didn't see the need to put me to so much trouble. I couldn't argue with her.

Turning to return the phone to its cradle, I saw only five minutes had passed. It seemed an eternity. I contemplated calling in sick so I could dream of that vision of loveliness but reason took over. I knew I'd cope better if I kept busy.

The week passed in a haze. How I managed to keep up appearances I'll never know but I don't think anyone suspected my turbulent state of mind, and body.

Friday finally arrived. I found myself full of frenetic energy all day. Never had I been so excited about a date. I lived through it a million times that day, rehearsing in my mind what we would do, what we would say, what she would wear. I must confess I had her in all sorts of exotic outfits, each more outlandishly seductive than the previous one and then felt ashamed for my preoccupation. I was beginning to think of her in terms of an object of desire, ignoring her very capable mind, concentrating only on the perceived exquisite pleasure I would experience in her presence. No woman deserved that, but I couldn't help myself.

Five o'clock slowly came around and I could leave. I caught the first bus home and walked into my townhouse a scant half hour later. Now, what to wear? We were only going down the road to the corner pub, and it really wasn't a very classy joint. Nevertheless, I was conscious of a desire to please that I had truly never before experienced with another human being. Besides, I was sure she would be dressed to kill and I didn't want to be a disappointment to her.

I didn't have much time. Paula prized punctuality above all other qualities. It was her parting shot before she spun off last Saturday night, so I could guess at its importance to her.

The drabness of my wardrobe appalled me. My clothes reflected my character - my business character anyway. I wore my best suit to the previous function. Only a pauper would dream of wearing the same suit twice in a row! I finally settled on a pair of black dress trousers, a cream silk shirt and a paisley tie. The tie I threw in at the last minute because I didn't want to look like a waiter! I gave my shoes a quick polish, laid everything neatly on the bed and wandered into the kitchen to grab myself a bite to eat.

I couldn't eat all day; I was so excited. Even now, with my stomach growling incessantly I could hardly eat. I forced a sandwich and a glass of juice down.

The chiming of the lounge clock reminded me time was passing. It was seven o'clock. I couldn't believe it had taken me so long just to decide what to wear and grab a bite to eat. I still hadn't showered and that was something I liked to take a bit of time over. I was so grateful she only wanted to meet me down the road and perhaps a little surprised as she lived on the North Shore while I slummed it on the South. If she wanted to meet anywhere else I'd have a hard time getting there on time.

I hurried through my ablutions as quickly as I could and not for the first time, blessed my parents for their forethought in endowing me with short wavy hair that required the minimum of fuss to keep neat and tidy. I was going to shave, but hoped the dated Don Johnson five-o'clock-shadow look would be impressive. It certainly saved time. At a quarter to eight, I was ready. A cursory glance in the hall mirror confirmed my handsome state of bachelor-hood and I couldn't help grinning to myself. Man, I looked good! I just knew Paula would be impressed.

I sauntered the two blocks down Crown Street and strode into the pub on the corner at five to eight. My eyes scoured the occupants of the already crowded bar. The night to go out is Friday, and although this was my local pub the sheer volume of Friday night clientele always surprised me.

I couldn't see her, but then I was early. I ordered a vodka and tonic and took it to the corner booth where I could watch the entrance. Then, more for something to do with my hands than because I actually wanted one, I lit a complimentary cigarette from the packet in the holder on the wall. I'm not a habitual smoker, having all but given up the dirty habit months ago, but I was so nervous. I was meeting Paula, for heaven's sake. The most beautiful woman I knew. I was getting on to thirty and had most of the things I wanted. I owned the townhouse on Crown Street and everything in it. My car, while not a Porsche, was sufficient for my needs. I had a good job, paying a terrific salary and there was even room for upward movement. I didn't have a special person to share all that with and truthfully, I never felt I wanted to until last Saturday night.

Paula. She was so beautiful. I just couldn't get her out of my head. If I had thought about it, she would be exactly the woman I'd been looking for all my life. I could see our children - that's how besotted I was. I could see little redheaded girls flouncing around in beautiful dresses dutifully turning their angelic faces to mine for a kiss from Daddy. Handsome, black-haired boys with curls dressed in tiny suits parading for their mother to praise their manly prowess. Yes, that would be my life with Paula.

I had long-since finished my cigarette and my drink was now more melted ice than anything. My watch showed me it was eight-thirty. Half an hour late! Maybe Paula prized punctuality in others, but found it unnecessary in her. I chided myself for my churlishness. Then it hit me. What if she'd had an accident? She could be lying bruised and broken by the side of the road, waiting for someone to come along and rescue her. That could be me, her Knight-In-Shining-Armour. And she would be my Damsel-In-Distress.

Acting on impulse, I left my seat and went to the phone booth in the lobby. I dialed the number for the nearest hospital and hung up before the connection went through. I didn't know her last name, or anything much about her. Just that she was Paula, and beautiful. I couldn't call any hospital about a person I hardly knew.

Back at the bar, I ordered myself another vodka and tonic. I needed something to help me think, and something to do other than worry. I downed that one in record time and ordered another. Some loud-mouthed under-age drinkers had overtaken my booth so I clung to the corner of the bar, gulping my third drink and gazing at the door. It's interesting the type of people that frequent establishments such as these. The clientele ranged from factory workers relaxing after a long week, still in their work clothes, to couples and singles either on dates, or attempting to form attachments. Then there was me. I began to believe I may have been stood up, and ordered a double vodka to compensate.

I thought it was too good to be true! While I'm not the world's worst looking male, I'm certainly no Greek Adonis. What was I thinking? How could someone as perfectly proportioned as Paula possibly see anything in me? She was merely having a bit of sport, and I was her victim. Waves of humiliation swept over me and I felt my face redden. Must be time for another double.

And then I saw her. She wasn't Paula, though she

was nearly as beautiful. She was much like a younger sister version of Paula - all the charm but without the polish. Sitting alone at a table for two littered with the previous occupants' glasses, ashtrays and chip packets that had been pushed to one side sat a very attractive woman. In my alcoholic haze I saw her look at me. Our eyes met and I could feel the heat of the moment even from that distance. Her eyes beckoned me, so I went.

I shoved my way through the crowd to find her expressive eyes following my progress until I reached her table. She indicated with her eyes that I take a seat. I did. She was not as stunning up close, but still presentable. And she was here, not God only knows where having a little chuckle to herself at my expense.

I opened my mouth to speak, intending to have a little fun myself rather than wallow in self-pity. Then I froze. On the wall behind her was a poster, advertising a popular local cover band's appearance here at my local Surrey Hills pub on the corner of Crown and Albert Streets next Friday night.

This was quite a normal thing to see in a pub, but there was something else on that poster that caused me to tremble like a baby, break out in a cold sweat and feel ill from the top of my head to the tip of my toes. It was the venue for the band's performance tonight: **The Pub On The Corner, PITT Street, The City.**

Passage of Time

There was nothing she liked better to do than to sit on the deck, watching the world go by. Amanda Robotham relaxed on a deck chair at the stern. James Robotham steered aft.

The gentle lapping of the water against the narrow boat and the hazy warmth of the dappled sunlight lulled her to a state of complete relaxation. She could have read a book, or prepared some culinary delight for their supper, even perhaps finish that crossword that had stumped her now for a whole month but today she opted to do none of that. She nursed her Yorkshire Gold, tea and filtered out the sound of the diesel engine, preferring to hear instead the tweets of birds in the trees lining the canal tow path and the rhythmic lapping of the water.

It was just over the cusp of the height of summer

on this idyllic July afternoon and James had decided to take the barge for a leisurely cruise down the canal to Leeds – just to keep the motor ticking, he had said, and, although she had thought perhaps she would like to pop into the supermarket for some supplies, she was content to relax.

It was a life she had once dreamed of in another time and place. James was once a high flyer in London's financial district, affectionately called "The Square Mile" and he and Amanda had met when she was Assistant to the Clerk of the Court. James was new to the Stock Exchange at that time and had needed her help to lodge some legal documents. He was taken aback by her sweet kindness, a rare commodity in the London girls at the time, and had shown his gratitude for her assistance by asking if he could meet her after work for a coffee. She had agreed and the rest was history.

The years had been kind to them; it was only when they looked at the old photographs that the ravages of time became obvious in the lined faces and greying hair. Still, they couldn't complain. They had their health, had retired early enough to enjoy their twilight years, and were now enjoying their freedom, giving up the London home for a life on the canal.

She had been happy enough in her role at Court until James's career had taken off and they had made the decision that she would give up her job and instead work for him. Events Manager was a fancy title and with his need to entertain his high-flying clientele, she was kept busy enough. During her quiet moments she caught up on her reading, exercised rigorously and took cookery classes. She rivalled some world-class chefs in the quality of the dishes she prepared for their guests when they entertained at home. She learned about wines and what wine would go best with what dish. James was often told it was his wife's influence that sealed the deal on many occasions.

There comes a time for some when the trappings of wealth are no longer a driving force in life and once James realised this, he took stock of his personal investments, saw he had plenty to see them through to the end and decided it was time to call it quits.

For a while they continued to live in their city house, continuing to entertain friends and acquaintances from their former life, James keeping his hand in on the investment scene until that fateful day, a few days shy of his fifty-second birthday

It was a balmy summer's day, not unlike today, and they had invited some friends over for a relaxed afternoon on the terrace. Amanda had opted to serve a barbecue and had enlisted her usual help from the village to assist her with the preparations.

The barbecue was lit earlier and was now down to those lovely hot coals that are so perfect for cooking on and the salads and desserts were all on ice, ensuring they stayed crisp and fresh. Amanda had just finished overseeing the finishing touches when she heard a commotion coming from the coach house.

James had wanted to show off his newest acquisition, a 1965 Ford Mustang to restore, but had simply collapsed, bringing down a good portion of the workbench with him.

Needless to say the party was cancelled and James spent the next few weeks in hospital and then the months that followed recovering from a major heart attack.

This was the wake-up call they needed and once James had recovered, they sold the house, put the contents of the workshop including the Mustang in storage, and retired to the canal.

The contrast from high-flyer with parties every other weekend to just the two of them on a 62 foot narrow boat was stark, yet in all honesty, it was probably even bigger than they really needed. It was toasty warm in winter with the pot-belly stove in the 'living room' providing a form of central heating to the whole boat. In summer, opening the windows brought the outside in with the smell of cut grass along the towpath and of flowers that bloomed from the spring to the end of summer, releasing their scent as the sun warmed them.

If it became too warm, they could simply move along the canal until they reached a shady spot and moor there. In winter they'd reverse the process, mooring in the sunshine when the air outside was chilly.

And so to today, James and Amanda floated aimlessly along the canal, James at the rudder,

Amanda perched in her deck chair, their silence companionable and soothing. They had no plans other than to enjoy the afternoon, possibly finding a new place to moor for the night.

Amanda woke from a short nap to the sound of squeals, laughter and barking dogs. Her nap had obviously been for some time as they had left the countryside behind and were now approaching the Oddy Staircase at Leeds.

A couple were sitting on the grass beside the tow path, two of their children chasing each other along the water's edge, running up the hill and back to where their parents sat. They giggled as their puppy followed them, yapping at their heels. A third child was sitting by herself with a scattering of clover flowers beside her, creating a chain out of them. She called over to her little sister, who came running, eyes shining at the flower tiara her sister placed on her head.

"Ooh, it's so nice, like," she said, prancing about like a princess. She then left off playing with her brother and sat at the water's edge. She grinned up at Amanda as the narrow boat passed, crawling now as they neared the first of the two locks that would take them down a few feet to the next level. Amanda grinned back and gave a little wave.

She loved the carefree nature of children and felt a little twinge that they had never had any of their own. It was not really something they had planned, this childless state, but as the years went by, it was less likely that it would ever happen and neither James nor Amanda felt any need to pursue this.

She sighed, stretched and made her way through the narrow boat to the 'engine room', where James was tending the rudder.

"Hello, Love," he said, watching his wife stroll through the boat towards him.

"Thought you might need a hand with the locks," she said, feeling a little guilty that he had already worked a few of them on his own while she snoozed. "You could have asked me to help, you know." She gave him a peck on the cheek and snuggled into his chest, feeling the calm, steady beat of his heart, grateful beyond measure that it was still there.

"I know, Love," he murmured into her hair, one hand stroking her bare arm, the other manoeuvring the long boat to the water's edge, ready to lightly moor her as he went to work the gates. "I was going to ask for your help, but you were so peacefully snoring."

"I was not snoring!" she exclaimed, knowing full well she probably was, and feeling just a little mortified that her vulnerability had been exposed to anyone out for a stroll along the tow path.

James chuckled lightly, the sound reverberating through his chest and straight into her heart. She grinned – not that he could see, of course. Leaning back, she looked up into his eyes.

"So, then Mr Robotham. Shall I work the lock?"

He released her and watched as she leapt out of the boat. No one would have put her at pushing a half-century and he was grateful that time had been so kind to her. He would have loved her even if she looked every minute of her years, though. She was his anchor in the storm.

James manoeuvred the narrow boat closer to the lock and closed the throttle completely, leaning out to throw the rope over the bollard.

Amanda spun the flywheel to open the gate, allowing James to guide the narrow boat into the lock. Once he was safely in, she closed the gate behind him and sauntered to the next gate, opening the sluice gates that would allow the water in the lock to drop to the level of the canal below, effectively giving the narrow boat a safe passage down the stream. She was fascinated with the engineering that made it possible for them to travel so far along the waterways of England, seeing so much. It was definitely a different view of the country than that seen from the motorways.

She had just finished her task when she felt a tug at her trousers.

"Excuse me, lady," said the little girl wearing the clover flower tiara, "can I look on your boat?"

"Oh, well, you'll have to ask your mam," she stammered. Children were creatures she admired at a distance, although this one was particularly sweet.

"Gemma!" The girl's mother ran over to them,

snatching the child's hand. "Don't bother the lady!"

"Erm, she's no bother, really," Amanda said. "She was asking if she could have a look on the boat."

"Oh, I'm so sorry. She's a little precocious, I'm afraid." Gemma's mother grabbed her hand again as it became obvious she was going to pull on Amanda's trousers again.

Amanda grinned, "Really, it's fine with me, if you're okay with it. Erm, you're all welcome to have a look if you like."

She felt a little out of sync from the real world. The past few months travelling on the canals had shown her a more relaxed pace and it was surprising how quickly she had become accustomed to its just being her and James. Little Gemma's contact was really the first intimate contact she'd had from other people for ages and although she felt a little awkward, there was a stirring in her heart that wanted to reach out to these people, little Gemma in particular.

"Oh! Well, I'm sure the children would love that! Thank you so much." She beckoned for her husband and older children to join them. "We can have a look around their canal boat. I've always wanted to ..." She trailed off, awkwardly, darting a look at Amanda who simply grinned at her.

"We'll have to wait until the lock empties and we can move the boat out," she said, perching herself comfortably on the arm. Gemma climbed up beside her, face beaming with excitement.

"Do you acksherly live on it? What's it like? Can you go real fast? Where's your kids?

"Hush, Gemma!"

"It's fine, she's just curious! I do live on the boat, Gemma, but I haven't always. I used to live in a big house in London, but this is much nicer, don't you think? We can't go fast – nice and slow." She ignored the question about kids.

With the level of the lock now equal to the lower level of the canal, she opened the gate and once James had guided the boat through, she closed it all again.

"We have visitors!" she said, ushering the family aboard.

James raised his eyebrows, questioning.

"This is Gemma. She asked if she could see what the boat's like. This is her mam ... Sorry, how rude of me. I'm Amanda and this is my husband, James."

"Chloe," said Gemma's mother. "Gemma, you know. This is my husband, Frank, and our two older children, Frank Junior and Emily."

Frank Junior was holding the puppy, who squirmed in his arms, eager to be let free. Frank Junior did not oblige.

The boat suddenly seemed a little crowded to Amanda, but not unpleasantly so.

"It's not a big boat, and there's not really all that much to see!" Amanda led them through the 'spare room' which they used for storage, rather than an extra couple of births, through their bedroom, which thankfully she was in the habit of tidying every day, to the kitchen / diner / living space.

Her guests took in the warm polished wood, plush carpet, comfortable two-seater sofa with matching armchairs. Her brother and sister stood politely, looking around while Gemma ran from one feature to the next, opening cupboard doors, exclaiming at the little kitchen sink, fridge and cooker, plonking herself on the sofa, and then climbing onto the back of the sofa to push aside the curtains, revealing the windows.

"Ooh, circles," she exclaimed, peering through the windows at the view outside. It was no different to what she had seen outside, but her excitement at this new experience was intoxicating.

"It's like a floating caravan – only bigger," Chloe said, nudging her husband. "Do you think we can get one?"

"You can go more places in a caravan," he said.

James chuckled, "That's probably true, but this way you get to enjoy the scenery while you travel. Believe me, it's a lot easier to navigate these locks than to drive for hours on the motorway."

"It takes so long!"

"We're in no rush." James grinned at Amanda. "One day you'll appreciate the slower pace, but canal life isn't for everyone." Amanda grinned back.

"Well, thanks for showing us around. I know you've given my wife ideas, but I think for now we'll stick with bricks and mortar and solid ground!"

The family traipsed back off the boat and James and Amanda went on their way.

They moored just before the Leeds #1 lock.

"Shall we have our tea here?"

"Eating out or in?"

"Not fussed. Depends on you, really. Do you want to cook?"

"Chauvinist!"

James grinned at her. "You're such a great cook, though. If it were up to me, we'd be having beans on toast."

"Nothing wrong with that! I'll do us some bangers and mash for our tea."

They ate in companionable silence, enjoying the peace and quiet of the evening. After tea, they cleared it all away and wandered hand in hand to the forward deck.

"We've got a great life, haven't we," Amanda said, holding the hand he casually draped over her shoulder.

They stood together, watching the sun set over the canal as the sky darkened and the moon rose.

"Indeed we have," James murmured. "And long may it continue!"

Scammed

I never saw it coming. I hadn't considered an early retirement, but now it's been thrust on me and I don't like it.

I've enjoyed my work. Over the years I've met many new and varied people and, if I do say so myself, I've managed to build a pleasant rapport with each of my clients.

Online businesses were all the rage and I managed to cash in on the trend and turn my talents into a very successful internet business. I've been doing this now for, well, it's really only been five years, but during that time I've gone from a two-bit, down-on-his-luck orphan who didn't have two coins to rub together to what I am today – or what I was yesterday! Well, life's a gamble, and most of my gambles have paid off big time!

But now that it's all over, all I'm left with are my memories. And what memories!

Sandy was such a nice girl. She was my first. I went on to an internet dating site and it was love at first sight. She was lovely and sweet, and had a philandering husband. I told her how I thought men like that deserved nothing and that someone as pretty as her deserved better. She was pretty, I guess, but to be honest, I've seen much prettier. However, I thought we got on very well and to tell you the truth, I think she really liked me a lot. I wish things could have been different between us, but fate intervened in the form of her husband coming back and that put an end to that one! Still, we had a good time, and for just a moment – well, a month or so – it was a very, how shall I put this ... Lucrative seems such a dirty word when speaking of matters of the heart, but there's no getting away from it; it was a lucrative relationship.

And Jennifer! She was pure class. Not my normal type if I'm honest. She was drop-dead gorgeous in a Vogue magazine cover sort of way. Very titillating! We met online, and I virtually wined her and dined her into my heart. And I do mean virtually! Unfortunately, we never did get to meet in person. After a couple of months she said she was tired of my demands. Demands?! Whatever could she mean? I offered her a great time, fantastic dream, and we all know there's no such thing as a free lunch, don't we? And I didn't ask for much ... only enough to pay for my mother-in-law's chemotherapy. Hard-hearted bitch! Well, it was probably just as well we'd never met. I would have showed her up and no Vogue model wants to be seen with a bloke who's better looking than she is.

Who else? Oh yeah, Samantha. You know, I'm surprised I can remember their names. I'd get confused sometimes, but if ever I forgot who I was talking to, I could always call them "Baby". They liked that!

Anyway, Samantha was a looker, too, but in a different way. She was a bit on the plump side and had just divorced. Sam was raising her kids on her own, she says without support from her ex! Come on! We all know the Child Support Agency makes them pay through the nose. I reckon she was secretly loaded, but she says she was poor. She showed me pictures of her house. Rented, but still better than what I'm used to. Anyway, she managed to help me out of a tight spot. She said that helping me out meant she couldn't buy new shoes for her kids, but I told her I'd pay her back. It wasn't my fault my mother-in-law's chemotherapy treatment had to be paid for. Again.

Well, that one ended in disaster. I offered her a free trip to Florence for my mother-in-law's funeral. The chemo didn't work this time, but after she'd booked the tickets for me, I couldn't get to the Western Union Office to send her the money. She didn't take that too well, and I've never heard from her since. Shame. I would have liked to show her around Florence! After the funeral, of course. We could have turned it into a real holiday.

Amanda was a real piece of work. She saw me as her ticket to the good life. I'm not sure how she came to that conclusion. It could have been the photographs of some minor Hollywood starlet's property in Malibu I sent her. Is it my fault she thought it was my place? She turned really nasty when I told her my children were ill and I wasn't able to ask my CO for leave and could she send me the airfare so I could just leave my post in Afghanistan to be with my children, who were being looked after by my late wife's mother in Edinburgh, who herself was quite ill. She ranted and raved at me over Skype and I almost severed the connection, I was shaking so much. Laughter, of course. Lucky I could mute her, and seeing as my web cam 'isn't compatible with hers', she couldn't actually see me anyway.

I had a close call with one of my ladies. Come to think of it, I wonder if it was Jill who gave the game away. How was I supposed to know her ex used to be in the Forces! I tried the Afghani-scam on her and she just told me how she knew she could do nothing to get my CO to give me leave, and reminded me I'd face court martial or worse if I went AWOL. She suggested I apply for leave on compassionate grounds – said it almost worked for her ex when she was in hospital miscarrying their first child – and that, although COs often come across as hard and unfeeling, they're human, too, and understand things like this. I had to do a lot of back-tracking on that one. It ended, though, when she refused to respond to my conversation requests.

Or it might have been the computer-savvy one, Sarah, the one who told me it didn't matter what computer she was using for Skype; whether the web cam worked or not had to do with my own computer. She offered to send me to her son next time I was in the country. She said he was a Mac Expert, and would have the cam working for me in no time. It nearly all came unstuck when she asked me how long I'd been in Bahrain when I'd told her I was in Sydney. I thought I'd covered my tracks well, but she managed to track me down in cyberspace. We were still talking the day they came to take me away!

Anyway, I could go on and on about the lovely ladies I've met along the way, but the end result is that I've now taken early retirement, involuntarily, and I'm not happy about it.

Well, what have we here! Now, this is one gorgeous woman walking towards me as we speak. The uniform accentuates her voluptuous body and she carries herself really well. "McIntyre" is blazoned across her right breast. The left breast remains nameless. A few blond strands have escaped the austere hair style covered by the green beret she wears. With a lick of make-up to accentuate those high cheek bones and seductive smoky grey eyes, she'd be a real looker. I've always been partial to authoritative women. I know you'd find that hard to believe considering what I've just told you, but there's something alluring about khaki trousers, a wide utility belt and a rifle slung over the shoulder. What a turn on! A rather mousy, non-descript woman accompanies her.

"Mr Stevens? Come with me."

"Sure thing, Baby." I give her a wink, ignoring her companion, and she gives me a cold, hard stare back. I shiver with anticipation. Retirement may not be so bad after all, if she's going to be here with me.

I follow her through the concrete corridors and past grated doors through which my new friends peer, whistling and cajoling my new conquest as she leads the way to my retreat.

All too soon our journey is over. Her companion hands me a bundle of clothes, a towel, and a toiletry pack and Khaki Trousers McIntyre unlocks the door to my room.

"I hope you'll be comfortable here, Mr Stevens." I'm not sure if she means it. Her voice is certainly not very welcoming – more stiff and formal, a bit like the starched khaki uniform she is wearing.

"Please, call me Ben," I say, grinning at her.

A raised eyebrow betrays her contempt. She gives me another cold stare, shoves me non-too-gently into my room and the door clangs shut. The key turns in the lock.

"Your new room-mate will fill you in on the routine." And then she was gone. I watched her as she marched back the way we'd come.

Retirement! Well, I've always been resourceful. Maybe I can use my talents here and build a comfortable life for myself. Maybe I'm only semi-retired!

I turn to my new room-mate and grin.

"How'd you like to make a few bucks on the side?"

.

The Recital

I heard the music as soon as I entered the cottage. It was Fur Elise played on an old Honky Tonk piano, an echo from my childhood.

I took the few steps to the door leading to the parlour and half-expected to see myself sitting at my great grandmother's old piano, stumbling over the chromatic scale, relief as I returned to the familiar motif. But the room was devoid of the human element. All that was there was an old piano wearing its tattered dust cover, flanked by a plump sofa and armchairs. The whatnot in the corner held a lifetime of memories in the form of trinkets collected over the years, some I had given her, and photographs of her children, grandchildren, and a spattering of great grandchildren occupied every available shelf, ledge and wall space.

I stepped into the room and the music skipped a beat, as if I had disturbed the ghostly pianist mid-recital. Nothing about the room had changed. I must have disturbed more than the pianist because the room was suddenly bathed in dancing, dusty light rays as the summer sun peaked through the cracks in the curtains. I didn't want to disturb the room, nor the memories just stepping inside the cottage had evoked in my head.

***

"I woke up to organ music and thought I had died and gone to heaven!" Grandma popped her head in the room as I practised the hymns for the morning service. I wasn't a good organist, not by a long shot, but I think I was the only one in the congregation who could actually play at least one-handed with the occasional left-hand note strategically thrown in. I had no idea what they did before I arrived, but now it seemed I was indispensable.

"Funny, Grandma!" I said. "I didn't mean to wake you. Just wanted to make sure I could play these hymns."

She shook her head, smiled and laid her hand on my shoulder.

"It was a lovely way to wake up."

I smiled at the woman who had taken me in when I had felt the need to leave my family at the tender age of seventeen. She was my paternal grandmother; I had not had too much to do with her growing up, simply because my father had died when I was a baby and my mother had remarried. I'm not sure why this meant that my sister and I, with the exception of a yearly visit to the house at Cabbage Tree Point, didn't get to see much of our father's family, but that's just the way it was. Consequently, although we knew we had uncles and cousins and we knew their names, we didn't really know them.

However, I was there then, making up for lost time. I spent so many weekends catching up with my cousins, meeting the younger ones for the first time. And for the first time I began to feel that I had family outside the dysfunctional one I grew up in. I began to understand where I came from, who I was and the people who had shaped the life of, or had been shaped by, the father I had never known.

I remember one day Grandma was out and I was home alone. We had since retrieved the old piano from friends who were supposed to be looking after it for me when my family had moved to New Zealand. Grandma's mother had had the piano brought over from her home in England to her new home in Australia, and shortly after my eighth birthday, I inherited it. The piano was already old by then, and the ivory keys had yellowed with age. Its original candelabra had long been removed but the mahogany finish had been preserved and was lovingly polished by me on a weekly basis.

However, my piano's time on their verandah had taken its toll. Although protected from direct rain, it was certainly not protected from the damp and humidity of a Queensland climate. The beautiful ivory keys had been chipped and broken, and they had been drawn on. It was clear there had been an attempt to clean it off, but the purple texta remained. The sanctity of the elephant's sacrifice, although acceptable in the days of the piano's creation, was desecrated by these children and the parents who left them to it.

I digress. I was home alone and playing a few songs on the piano, or trying to. I gave up on the pieces I was practising and decided to see what I could remember of Fur Elise. I had first heard one of the older boys at Church playing it when I was a pre-teen and I was fascinated by it. It is a simple enough tune, and even quite simple to play, the motif, anyway, but for some reason, the music spoke to me like no other piece ever had.

I was engrossed in my playing and so didn't notice the dogs barking, or the front door opening, then I was suddenly aware of my grandmother standing there beside me. Her hand gently touched my shoulder and tears streamed down her face.

"Grandma, what's wrong?" I asked, thinking the worse. A death in the family, perhaps. She just shook her head and composed herself.

Then, taking a deep, ragged breath, she said, "I thought it was your dad playing." Another ragged breath. "It was his favourite piece of music - he played it all the time."

"Oh, Grandma! I had no idea. I'm so sorry."

"Don't be," she said. "It was lovely to hear it again." She sniffed and smiled. "He was lovely, your dad. I wish you could have known him."

"Me, too," I murmured, and although his brothers and mother had told me so much about him, I still yearned to know the man he had been, or would have become had he lived.

I only stayed with Grandma for a short six-month period and then life took over. I still went to visit her, and even had another short stay with her, and I felt our relationship had continued to grow.

Many years passed. Too many and I'm ashamed to say my visits became less frequent. My own dreams of being a concert pianist were swallowed up in the day-to-day life of looking after children and earning a living. I was never going to be able to devote the time necessary to perfect my technique and in either case, I would never remember the pieces without having the sheet music in front of me. I remember hearing my grandmother play the old war favourites - all by ear - and any time we were somewhere with a piano, she would always say:

"Play us a tune, Sammy!"

I would always remind her that I couldn't play anything without the sheet music. She said she was jealous of my ability to read music. I was jealous of her ability to play by ear. I could pick out the tune of a favourite song, but Grandma played beautiful accompaniments as well as the tune. I had certainly not inherited that talent.

Again, I digress; probably because of my shame in not keeping in touch.

It was not long after the tragedy that was September 11, 2001. Although not directly affected, even as far away as in Australia, the ramifications of this heinous act were felt world-wide.

Grandma was now in her eighty-second year and she had been granted her wish to see in the new millennium. I wondered then, and still do wonder, what she thought of the way the world was going. She had lived through the death of her parents, the death of one son and the death of her husband. More recently, she had lived through the death of her beloved sister, and I had visited her around the time of my great aunt's passing.

Grandma had described what I can only suggest was either an out of body experience or an extremely vivid dream, in which she said she was in the room with her sister when she died. Grandma lived a good 200 miles from the hospital where Aunty Rose died and by this time, she had given up driving.

I told her I thought she was blessed to have had that experience. She looked at me as if I had lost my mind.

"It was frightening," she said.

"I know," I said, "but you had the chance to say goodbye."

She thought for a minute, which seemed an eternity, and then nodded.

More years sped by. I never saw Grandma again after that visit and fifteen days following the collapse of the Twin Towers in New York City, my grandmother passed away peacefully in her sleep.

And now, here I am, standing just inside the parlour of my grandmother's home, listening. The old piano died a long time ago and a shiny new one took its place. Yet, underneath the shroud, I could hear the strains of that old honky tonk piano, sometimes playing Fur Elise, the song I had interrupted, but, as I gently perched on the edge of the over-stuffed sofa thinking back on the life of an extraordinarily wonderful woman, I heard the old war songs she used to play so well.

Finally, as the sun set on that day I heard the final song: "We'll meet again".

And then the tears flowed.

.

ARTICLES

Close Call: Excerpts From A Biography of a WWI Veteran

I expected to see an old man and that's exactly what I saw.

Eric Abraham celebrated his 102nd birthday on 20 April 2000 with thousands of school children across the Brisbane area. It was a party to remember. Not only was it Eric's 102nd birthday, but five days would mark the 85th anniversary of the ANZAC landing at Gallipoli. It was a celebration and a commemoration in just one week.

Beryl Wilson, Eric's companion, ushered me through the cottage at the RSL Veterans Home at Pinjarra Hills in Brisbane's west and out to the back veranda. A lively woman, possibly half his age but more likely a little older, she has one of those ageless faces. I didn't feel it polite to ask her age, nor what her relationship with Eric was. Some things are sacred. They left me with an impression of mutual respect. Eric refers to her as "the girl who looks after me". I was content to leave it at that.

What a magnificent view there was from the veranda! Eucalyptus gums covered the land for as far as the eye could see. The land rose gently to become a hill, towering over the valley in the distance. The air was a little hazy, but that only added to the atmosphere of the day. Beryl said Eric was tired, as I suspected he would be. It was already late afternoon by the time I could get in to see him. I had made the appointment weeks in advance, thinking by four he'd have had his nap and feel rested after the morning's ordeal. It was not to be. Since his first engagement that morning, the press had hounded him and I became only one more in a string of engagements. Another was scheduled after me.

Eric joined me on the back verandah. He didn't look 102, but he did look old. Then again, I had never seen a 102-year-old man before. I just know I'd seen much younger men who looked considerably older than Eric. There's no denying it. The four years spent in the Australian Imperial Forces went a long way to creating Eric, the man he is today. Even so, it was hard to identify the boy-soldier with the tired old man who sat before me, yet he was one and the same. A photograph of the soldier Eric sat on the verandah table, and on his suit jacket hung his medals, including the coveted Legion of Honour, France's highest honour. That was the ultimate proof.

***

It was late October of 1915. A brass band played in the town square where a crowd had gathered. Farm cockies, men and boys in everyday work clothes, carrying nothing but a duffle bag filled with their meagre possessions, milled around. Many had begun their march in Warwick. It was hard to believe, but once they left, most would never set foot on Australian soil again.

Still, it was a carnival atmosphere. There were speeches. "Step right up! Take the opportunity of a lifetime! See the World! Your country needs YOU!" The band played rousing melodies to get the blood pumping, children kicked up the dust, and young men grabbed their kit bags and joined the march. And women wept. A premonition? Perhaps.

From inside the Boonah Post Office, 17-year-old Eric Abraham heard the familiar strains of "God Save the King!" Stirring within his breast was a seed of patriotism. In a daze, the young postal worker, who was very familiar with Morse code, left the office. He followed the music to the town square where the excitement was as intoxicating as a drug.

"I had no intention of enlisting," he said, "but the National Anthem! Oh my Godfather! Before I knew it I was signing on the bottom line." And so he joined the Dungaree March in the final days of October 1915, enlisted in Ipswich in November and continued on to Enoggera.

Finally, basic training was over! He was now

Private Eric Kingsley Abraham, 5th Division Signal Company, Australian Imperial Forces. How proud he was, with the invincibility of youth. He thought it was the best thing he had ever done in the 17 and a half years of his life. Would he regret his impulsiveness? At least, unlike many others, he lived.

***

"Oh, my God! What am I doing here?" Eric muttered to himself. 'Here' was Sausage Gully on the Somme in France in August 1916. It was a far cry from the days of basic training at Enoggera, the trip on the *Star of Victoria*, or even the extra training in the deserts of Egypt. This was the real thing.

He and a mate were carrying rations to the troops. It was only his first day in the field. The Sinai had not prepared him for this. Picking his way gingerly over the muddy ground, Eric lugged the sand bag full of tins onto his shoulders. His mate had the stew in a pot the soldiers affectionately called a dixie. Suddenly, gunfire erupted all around them.

"Shit!" he exclaimed, as his knees buckled underneath him. He tumbled to the bottom of the trench, drenched in sweat and stew, his mate following close behind.

Nearby laughter confused him. It was the last thing he expected to hear and he looked up into the blue eyes of a seasoned soldier.

"That was us, cobber," he said, tears of laughter scouring the grit from his face in crinkly lines. "Just wait 'til Fritz answers. Now, that's something to shit yourself over!"

Eric picked himself up and, mustering what dignity he had left, continued with his task.

Arriving back at the communications dugout, he plopped himself into a seat and held his face in his hands.

"What's up with you, Private?" his Sergeant asked.

He was silent for a long time.

"I'm not cut out for this," he finally muttered into his hands. "I lost it when our own troops fired at the Germans. What am I going to be like when they fire back?"

"Everyone feels like that the first time," the Sergeant replied. "It's terrifying. If anyone tells you different, he's either a liar, or he wasn't there. Or both."

What an introduction it was to the arena of war. The gunfire. The artillery rounds. The mud. Oh, dear God, the incessant mud. Some bright spark in Headquarters ordered the heavy guns, and even when shells demolished the irrigation pipes reducing the land to a swampy quagmire, the orders came to continue shelling. Explosions were lost in the mud. Weapons were lost in the mud. Men drowned in the mud. And other men looked helplessly on.

***

A bout of bronchitis and pleurisy early in the new

year of 1917 saw Eric's evacuation to England. His respite was brief. Recovery saw him back with his unit in France, back among the endless mud and the stench of death.

They laid duckboards across the worst mud holes to facilitate movement but it was still a messy business.

"It was sheer hell," remembers Eric. "Nobody told Fritz he shouldn't fly over the war-formed marsh lands. Nobody told Fritz to leave the poor buggers in the mud alone. Nobody thought to just pack it all in and go home."

For once it wasn't raining. Eric, with some rare time off, decided to take a walk. The day had a seaside holiday feel. It was a pleasant afternoon, the sun was shining and a gentle breeze kept the temperature comfortable. The insidious mud still dominated the landscape, though, making it necessary to walk along the duckboards. He imagined the war had ended and 'Pte Abraham' was just plain Eric, going about his business, probably on his way to meet with some French dame for a spot of afternoon tea. A plane flew overhead. Planes were always doing that. Most likely it was some sightseeing tourists getting a bird's eye view of the world and paying for the privilege.

Suddenly all hell broke loose. The tourists had changed their minds about sightseeing and decided to try target practice instead. Machine gun bullets struck the boards at his feet. His reaction was automatic, immediately diving off the boards into the quagmire - and staying there, very still. The target shooters decided to move their shooting gallery onward, believing him dead.

"You think I'm dead, ya bastard," he shouted to the long gone plane. "I'm just a lucky digger covered in mud!" He lay there a moment longer, heaved a sigh and shuddered. "Shit, that was close."

Eric picked himself up, and resumed his walk.

**

Death was never far away in the trenches. If you didn't sink and suffocate in the soggy earth, contract pneumonia, or die of festering wounds, a stray bullet was sure to find you eventually. Maybe even a mortar shell.

It was during the Battle of Passchendaele, also known as the Third Battle of Ypres on September 25, 1917. Fighting was unusually intense. Soldiers rotated their shifts so they always had fresh young ones at the front, with four days on and fourteen to recover. Eric wasn't that lucky. He and two sappers, Roy Hawke and Nick Walsh, were assigned 'round the clock shifts, to keep the communication lines open. There were always two on, while the third went back to the dugout to sleep.

Looking after the battalions, in the forward area, Eric had come on duty to relieve Roy.

"See ya tomorra, Kizzy." Roy tipped his hat to Eric as he left the tent with the Sergeant.

Hawke had only just stepped out when an explosion sounded outside the tent door. The force of the blast blew the candles out. Papers scattered everywhere and the relentless black ooze splattered everything.

"Shit, that was close," Nick said, running grimy hands through even grimier hair.

"Good God," exclaimed Eric. "Roy Hawke must have got that! Where's the Sarge?" He ran to the tent opening and looked out.

"There's a bloody big hole here, about 12 foot wide!" he shouted to Nick

Hawke and the Sarge were lying about two feet apart on the rim of the crater. The Sarge was unconscious but groaning. Blood flowed from Hawke's temple and a gaping hole in his chest oozed blood as well.

"How is everyone?" Nick shouted.

"The Sarge's OK. Hawke bought it, though."

"Did you check his pulse?"

"I've seen enough dead bodies to know one when I see one. No need to feel the bloody pulse."

Eric went over to the Sarge and patted him on his cheeks.

"What the hell happened?" the Sarge asked.

"A shell got you, Sarge," Eric answered. "Roy Hawke's dead."

Sarge shook his head and groaned again. "Bloody murder," he muttered.

"You okay?" Eric asked. Sarge said he was and Eric helped him back into the tent to relieve Nick. Now there was only the two of them to work the telegraph.

"Looks like we're it, eh Kizzy," Nick said when Eric came back in. Nick had tidied the place up enough to get to work. The candles were relit and the flickering light hid the filth that must surely still be there in the shadows.

Nick and Eric took turns sleeping in the communications tent and keeping the messages coming that night, sharing Eric's bedroll. It was a long night. In the morning, Nick went back to the camp to collect the rest of their stuff. He came back empty-handed.

"Kizzy," he said. "I can't find the bloody camp. I think I'm goin' mad."

Leaving the communications tent, they both went back to the camp. There was nothing there except a gaping hole, like the one where they found Hawke and the Sarge. Both young men looked at each other.

"You thinking what I'm thinking, Kizzy?" asked Nick.

"I reckon," he replied. "If Roy hadn't bought it last night, either you or I would have been in there."

***

I looked at the lined face of the old man sitting in

front of me. He was tired from the day's activities and in need of rest, but there was strength there. I wondered where it came from.

"I know you survived physically, but how did you endure those horrid war days mentally," I asked.

There was a glint in his eye as he said, "It was the grace of God. I'm not a religious man. Certainly I've never been a regular churchgoer, but God had a plan for me. I don't know what it was, but I've been kept alive for something. God certainly moves in mysterious ways."

Eric Kingsley Abraham has lived a long and productive life. Where such experiences could have left him embittered, he has found purpose. He returned home from the war at age 21, a more sophisticated, powerful man. One of the last survivors of his generation, he has grown to become everyone's hero.

Bibliography

Australian War Memorial *Roll of Honour Database,*

http://www.awm.gov.au/database/roh.asp - *Accessed September 22, 2000*

Defence Force Records, *Private Eric Kingsley Abraham.*

http://www.minister.dva.gov.au/media/media/apr99/new.htm - *Accessed August 24, 2000*

Telford, P *2000, Transcript of Interview with Eric Abraham (April 20, 2000)*

Tieman, JS *1998, TPQ OnLine, Passchendaele. –*

http://trfn.clpgh.org/tpq/Ampray4.html *Accessed September 23, 2000*

Whittaker, Dr L, *ANZAC's Day*

http://www.terrax.org/projects/australia/anzac.html - *Accessed September 22, 2000*

Whittaker, Dr L, *Stories From World War One*

http://www.terrax.org/projects/australia/eric/eric.html - *Accessed September 22, 2000*

Flying Over The Enemy

Being shot down over Yugoslavia a year before the end of World War II was probably not high on anyone's 'to do' list, but that's what happened to Flight Officer Mervyn Bradford, an Air Observer with the Royal Australian Air Force.

At fifteen, Mervyn joined the Field Artillery Militia in the Wynnum/Manly district – and lied about his age to do so. Many of his mates went on to join the Australian Imperial Forces, as it was then known, but, with lofty visions of becoming a pilot, Mervyn joined the RAAF. The powers that be had other ideas, but he was still in the skies during the war.

As an Air Observer attached to the Pathfinders, it was Mervyn's crew's job to illuminate the sites for bombing, which he did using parachute flares. On one such flight, his plane was shot down, and though all survived, most were captured and sent to various prisons. Mervyn went first to a prison in Budapest, where he was constantly interrogated.

He was in a position to know many of the battle plans, and certainly knew the success or failure of some missions, having flown on them himself. However, in keeping with the Geneva Convention, he only ever stated his name, rank and service number, a fact that infuriated his captors. They wanted him executed as a spy, but despite starvation, threats and cajoling, he stuck to his guns.

His stint in solitary confinement was a nightmare of bug infested bedding, a narrow room with barely enough space to stretch, yet an endless ceiling above him and a windowless opening high above for ventilation. Food was rationed at a small piece of bread every day. "On Sundays, it was covered in caraway seeds," Mervyn says.

Conditions were barbaric, but tolerable.

Not surprisingly, he lost a lot of weight in Budapest.

Life in the German camps was marginally better – at least they were clean!

"It was a happy day – relatively – when we were taken over by German troops and marched to the shower room where we had our first clean-up for months," Mervyn recalls.

They were shipped off in a boxcar to Stalag Luft 3 at Sagan (now called Zagan), made famous by the World War II classic movie, The Great Escape, where 55 prisoners escaped and evaded capture – for a while – and were eventually executed.

"That was about 12 months before we got there," he says. By the time his group arrived in Sagan, the war in Europe was almost over, and with Germany so badly bombed, Mervyn says there was nothing to help escapees along the way.

Mervyn says that although conditions in the German camps were harsh, they were nothing compared to the experiences of those captured by the Japanese.

Still, they were underfed, and having been starved for so long, Mervyn said he could eat just about anything. He could stomach what the POWs affectionately named 'fish cheese' due to its putrid smell, but it was the red and juicy blood sausage that he almost drew the line at.

Although many people believe a man uprooted from his family and loved ones is obsessed with women, Mervyn is quick to point out this is not so.

"Our female companions will be disappointed to learn that the main topic of conversation was FOOD, not women!"

He may seem flippant about it all now, but living the life of a POW, for however short a time, is nothing glamorous.

Mervyn hopes the young people will understand what the men of his generation had to do, and will recognise the sacrifices of those who made it home – and those who didn't – for what it was.

'We must remember and honour the supreme sacrifice made by so many of our mates. [In the light of recent terrorist events] the motto of the RSL is today even more relevant than ever: 'The Price of Liberty is Eternal Vigilance.'

Reluctant Hero

He downplays his experience as a prisoner of the Japanese in the Second World War, but through it all, he has emerged a survivor, one of the hordes of unsung men of his generation, heroes who fought for our freedom.

Craftsman Stanley Joseph Manning joined the Army in August 1941. At 24, he was neither the oldest nor the youngest Australian to join the battle, however, as fate would have it, he was not to spend too long at the front.

He was captured by the Japanese, and transported to Changi prison on the island of Singapore and from there, much of his time as a POW was spent working on the Thai-Burma railroad working from the Burmese side.

"They had us in different groups – I was in A-Force – and they got us to build the railway."

Life was not easy, and because of his Chinese ancestry and the traditional bad blood between the nations, his Japanese captors singled him out for mistreatment. Yet he survived.

'When you see so many die, and you're still alive, it reinforces your determination not to die. I had no wife or girlfriend back home, just my mother and my two sisters.'

When his sisters heard he'd been captured, they gave him up for dead, but not his mother.

"Mum never varied in her belief that I was going to come home."

Stan might have spent the war years as a prisoner but he didn't just sit there and take it.

"I did what I could to defy them," he says, and though he offered no further details, his wife Pam mentioned his defiance at the physical exercises they were forced to do daily.

"He told me he used to stand at the back and pretend to do them," she says, but he paid for his insubordination! They made him stand out in front to make sure he did them.

He left Singapore in September 1944 and a week later, US submarines attacked the convoy of Japanese vessels. Thirteen ships in all were sunk from that attack.

Stan and a mate were on deck when the torpedoes hit their ship. They hid under a tarp for a while, drenched to the skin from the spout caused by the torpedo, but rather than panicking and jumping overboard, they made their way down to the galley and grabbed some rice and water. Then they jumped.

"The Japanese lost control over the prisoners. It was every man for himself. There were about 1300 prisoners on the ship. Most of them drowned."

Stan was in the water for days, hanging on to planks to keep afloat. Thankfully, Japanese depth charges searching for the elusive US subs kept the sharks away. He eventually made it onto one of the Japanese life rafts commandeered by his fellow POWs – after refusing to climb aboard a couple that were so overloaded only sheer will power kept the sea water out.

Finally, in the distance they could see a warship heading their way. Rescue was imminent. All in all, the US submarines that had caused the damage picked up 70 POWs; the Japanese rescued 60.

Stan was one of the 60. He spent the rest of the war in Japan, and even when the war was finally over, he had to wait to come home.

Stan is now bed-ridden from the effects of diabetes. His hearing and eyesight are not what they used to be, but his memories of his time as a POW are quite clear.

And yet, when one of his daughters recalled to him a story he had told her once before – of how he had somehow obtained a set of keys and unlocked some of his fellow POWs, using his Chinese ancestry to full advantage, he smiled a secret smile, and claimed he didn't remember!

Essay

Letters

Synopsis – Although Hallie is a fictional young woman from rural Ethiopia, her story could be that of any young child growing up in poverty today. Hallie's family was hit hard during the famine in the 1980's, but through the help of Suraya, her World Vision sponsor, and Hallie's own strong determination to succeed, she has risen from being the poor eldest daughter of a widow to a highly educated school teacher, teaching the younger children in the village Hallie called home for much of her young life.

Now she is older and wiser, she faces decisions common to many young scholars the world over. And yet her dilemma is so different. As a child sponsored through World Vision, she is expected to use her privileged position to the betterment of her village. For a time, Hallie was content to do this, but things are different now. These letters written by Hallie and

Suraya give us a glimpse into their world ...

January 25, 2004

Dearest Miss,

I thank you so much for your welcome letter. It has come at a time when, although I am well, I am feeling much heartache. I have so many decisions before me, and I do not feel capable of making them without receiving some advice from you. As my cherished sponsor, you have been a part of my life since I was a timid child of only ten. Actually, you have been a part of my life since my eighth birthday.

Did you know that was the day I first learned I was chosen to be a part of the World Vision program? If I had known then, how I would be faced with such a heart-rending decision, I do not know if I would have accepted your generous help. As it is, I am torn between a love of my country, my family – all I have ever known – and a burning desire to see more, do more, even be more.

When we first met, I was already doing better than I had hoped. My teachers marvelled at my enthusiasm for learning. I was like a sponge not yet at saturation point. Not only was I eager to learn all they had to teach me, but I also wanted to learn your words so I could write to you. My first letters must have been so difficult for you to read, but when your replies came, I flew to my teacher to have her help me to read them! I thought I had already learned so much, and yet I soon discovered just how much more there was to learn.

As I grew, I began to appreciate what I now had. At first it was just the new uniform, the books and pencils and how I could fit in with the other children in the school. My family's living standards improved as we received blankets, and an allowance to buy seeds to plant, and food to eat while our fledgling garden grew. A lovely couple came to help my widowed mother to better manage what little finances we had, and our little family prospered. But then it became more than that. I was no longer a sponge, but a patient awakening from a coma with a renewed sense of living, or a newborn child with a voracious appetite – not only for food which was plentiful now that we had learned to beat the famine – but also for sensual experiences, and love.

I began to be jealous of my time. I was no longer content to go to school, and then to return and teach my younger brothers. Any moment spent away from my books was a great hardship. I resented my family – felt burdened by them. And still I knew I was being unfair. I was so blessed by your generosity and felt obliged to repay you in some way.

Your letters to me stipulated that the best way I could repay you was to make something of myself. That I have tried to do a million times over. I finished my schooling, and obtained employment in the village school. The lessons I begrudged my younger brothers truly helped me there, as I related to the younger children of my village.

Now every moment I spent in the classroom with them was a godsend! I looked on their eager young faces and saw what my teacher must have seen in me all those years ago. There was a hunger that I simply cannot describe to you, being multiplied as it were by a factor of thirty. My heart swelled with joy at the thought that I could do for them what my teacher had done for me! What a turn-around from the selfish young girl I was! Yet after a few years I found I was no longer able to teach them. Sure there were still younger ones eager to learn, but the older ones completed studying what I could teach them, and left to go back to their former lives. With the extra knowledge they gained, their lives were not as frugal as before, but I knew they could benefit from so much more.

I decided to apply for a scholarship to another school where I could learn even more and then be able to pass on my greater knowledge to the students. My old teacher put in a good word for me, and as I have only recently found out, you did too. I am so grateful and feel even more indebted to you. I won the scholarship and with mixed feelings – a lot of excitement mingled with more than my fair share of fear and trepidation – I set off to Abote, boarding with a distant cousin of my late father's for a couple of years. I did so well; proving my thirst for knowledge had only grown stronger. I was offered a place at university, and of course, I accepted.

Now I have completed my Bachelor's Degree in Business Education and will soon graduate with honours. I have enjoyed my time at the University of Addis Ababa, but I want to learn more. Am I being selfish? Is it right for me to want so much? You have opened so many doors for me. I no longer have a life of eking out a meagre existence on the family farm to look forward to. I am no longer at the mercy of the elements, fighting famine and drought. I don't even have to teach anymore. I can be whatever I want to be. I find myself looking for further opportunities.

Just this morning I received in the post, along with your latest letter, an information pack for an American university. I want so much to go and see what I can be, but I feel I may be obliged in some way to go back to my village and help establish the new learning facility there. We were planning to integrate a new high school with a place where we can teach our parents some of the things we have learned.

I was once content simply to be. I want more than that now. I have seen a little of life outside my village. It's not all good, but I want it.

That is my dilemma. I'm hoping you will understand. Perhaps you will even be able to advise me. But I know you can never make my decision for me. For that I can rely only on what I feel is right.

Your loving and grateful 'child'

Hallie

February 15, 2004

Dearest Hallie,

When John and I decided to sponsor a child back in 1980 we never dreamed our 'child' would be such a success! All we hoped for was to save one poor starving child and if we could save her family, too, that would be a bonus. You have far exceeded our expectations. The work you have done with the young people of your village has more than paid back the debt you think you owe.

I'm not going to tell you what to do. You were right in saying it is your decision. But I want you to know how I feel.

When the shy ten-year-old girl wearing the bright blue dress first looked into my eyes, I saw a light I had never seen before. As you know, John and I have five children, and they are all successfully living their lives with children of their own. We sent them off to school with all the privileges they were accustomed to, and to a small degree, they were grateful for that. But you! It seemed to me that your chance for education meant so much more to you than theirs ever could to them. With pride you showed me your first efforts at writing, and as you stammered over the unfamiliar words in that old English primer, I felt a delicious shiver of expectation run throughout my whole body. I just knew you were special.

I sat in on your classes. The hours you kept were so odd; I felt I had to understand. Your teacher told me that as the eldest daughter, your home responsibilities were great. With your mother, you tended your younger brothers, kept the little house you lived in scrupulously clean and tended your fields. I know your little brothers helped, but as your mother was ill a lot of the time, the bulk of the responsibility fell on your young shoulders. And you were only ten! I think of my own daughter at ten and how little, comparatively, she was expected to do, and in some small way I began to understand how important my small sacrifice was to you. Who would have thought that such a small amount of money could accomplish so much? And yet my money was nothing compared to your effort.

I followed your progress through school, and when you were asked to teach the other village children, I felt so proud. Our sponsorship was supposed to end when you found employment, and though we stopped paying to you and switched to help another child, we still continued to write and through you and the friendship we developed with your old supervisor, we learned how you were doing. I was as proud as you were when you won that scholarship to go to the high school. Of course I put in a good word for you! Why wouldn't I? I could see how much education meant to you, and when you asked me what I thought, I immediately found out what I could do to help you. And then you came back and helped all those kids again.

I was sorry to hear of your mother's passing, and worried about you for a while, but you soon showed the world you were made of tougher stuff. And then you went to university! Now you tell me you're graduating soon.

Hallie, you are such a sweet and special young woman. You have given so much back to your community already, and I know you will continue to do so – whether you stay in Ethiopia or find your own way somewhere else in this wide world. I know you will make the decision that is right for you.

Good luck and God Bless,

I remain your devoted 'Miss',

Suraya

ABOUT THE AUTHOR

Originally from Australia, Phoebe now lives in West Yorkshire with her husband Ewen and two of her five children.

She has always loved the written word – but couldn't tell you who her favourite author is. She doesn't have just one! She reads anything from cereal packets through historical romances to Sci-Fi / Fantasy, and pretty much anything in between. She discovered Tolkien in her early twenties and more recently has read JK Rowling's Harry Potter series (a couple of times) and Stephenie Meyer's Twilight series. She even went through a crime stage, reading Nora Roberts and Patricia Cornwell, as well as a horseracing phase with Dick Francis. Basically, if it had words, she'd read it!

Her earliest childhood memories of writing include a ghost story she wrote in Year 4 and a humorous story involving her head teacher's fear of thunderstorms in Year 6. Sadly she no longer has copies of these and would have loved to revisit them to see how her style has developed over the years. She has a couple of novels in various stages of completion. In the meantime she offers this, her second collection of short stories, articles and essays.

Printed in Great Britain
by Amazon

59568454R00115